Harkworth Hall

L.S. JOHNSON

This is a work of fiction. All characters and events portrayed in this book are either fictitious or used fictitiously.

Traversing Z Press
San Leandro, California
www.traversingz.com

ISBN: 978-0-9988936-1-7
Library of Congress Control Number: 2017943456

Poetry excerpts are from "Ocean: An Ode, Concluding with a Wish," by Edward Young

TABLE OF CONTENTS

Upon earth there is not his like,
who is made without fear.
— Job 41:33

ENGLAND
THE NORTH
1752

CHAPTER I

The Birds

J first heard of Edward Masterson the day of the birds, though I forgot about them through much of what happened after. Indeed, in the moment, their strange flight was only a disturbing inconvenience, as it turned my father back from his walk to the village on laundry day.

My father was a gentleman of small, regular habits. He walked to the village twice each week, to gain news of the wider world and have two pints of ale before walking back. In winter, he had Mr. Simmons, who served as our steward as well as sometime butler and valet, drive him. But in the fine weather of late spring he would set off walking, in his plain suit but with his sword polished and ready should he meet any ruffians.

The rest of our little household—myself and Mr. and Mrs. Simmons; my poor mother had passed when I was young—would plan much around this simple outing, for the house was too much work for the Simmonses alone. My father made no objection to my helping with light chores such as dusting, but he had recently been infected with the disease of matchmaking, and he feared for my prospects should I develop a working woman's hands and complexion. His solution for our overworked staff was to simply hire more help as needed, but I often snuck into his study to review our account books and there was no surplus for such luxuries. Thus, I learned to separate want from necessity, and while other women my age were dancing at assemblies or practicing their needlework, I was scrubbing floors and learning to make pastry. I learned, and I learned as well to not reflect upon my circumstances, lest I fall into melancholy—and many days there was simply no time for such indulgence. As soon as my father left, I put aside my role as Caroline Daniels, landowner's daughter, and became Caroline Daniels, maid, stableboy, or whatever we needed me to be. Laundry especially was a daylong affair, and more than once we had sent Mr. Simmons out to delay my father so we could get the last damp pieces inside before he returned.

My father left, drawing the door closed behind him. I waited in the hall, seeing in my mind's eye his stout figure striding down the drive. Now he would pat his pockets, ensuring he had a shilling but little more, for he had once been robbed on his return and had a fine watch and several shillings taken off him. Now he would think about that watch, and touch his sword in reassurance. All was well and nothing was forgotten; he could enjoy his journey in peace, and we could set about our work. I counted to fifty, then with a deep breath seized the first laundry basket and began dragging it back to the yard—

—when I heard the terrible sound of the door swinging open again, and my father bellowing for Mr. Simmons. At once I dropped the basket, smiling brightly. My smile faded, however, when I saw the spatters on his hat and coat, including a red smear on his face.

"Are you all right? Did you fall?" I rushed towards him, thinking to stop any bleeding with my apron.

"Quite all right," he said. "Only the birds are going mad."

For a moment I stared at him, believing I misheard him, but then I saw movement in the sky past his shoulder. Birds of all sizes and shapes, flying at odd angles to each other but all heading inland. As I watched two collided, then set at each other with horrific shrieks and bared claws. Feathers drifted down as they fought.

"I've never seen anything like it. It's quite late in the year to be mating, and there are *gulls* up there. They usually stay close to the shore—" My father suddenly broke off, frowning at the laundry basket. "What are you doing with that laundry?"

"I was looking for a petticoat," I said quickly. "I cannot find it anywhere."

He gave me a suspicious look, but I was saved from further inquiry by Mr. Simmons appearing. As he fetched my father a fresh coat, I slipped past him and went out onto the drive. Dozens of birds filled the sky, and save for when their paths provoked a conflict, they were doing so in near silence, as if they needed all their strength to fly. But what were they flying towards—or were they fleeing something? I scanned the horizon: there was not so much as a cloud, not a hint of an incoming storm.

Above me two more birds crossed paths, and the larger one viciously raked the smaller. It tumbled to the ground, then carefully righted itself and began limping forward, still heading unerringly inland.

"Caroline, dear, don't distress yourself with such sights." My father took my arm and led me back to the house.

"But what could be causing it?" I asked, still craning my head. "Something has frightened them, something worse than a storm."

"They were probably startled by an animal—perhaps we have a wolf again. I'll ask in the village," he said. "Oh, and I forgot to tell you! I will be stopping at the Fitzroys' on my way home. I was thinking if Diana spends the season in town again, perhaps you could join her? A stay of some weeks will help you become more comfortable in society, and develop your acquaintanceships further."

And there were so many replies I wished to make, all at once. The Fitzroys were our closest neighbors, and Diana my oldest friend. Having both lost our mothers early, and without siblings, we had been for a time closer than sisters. The memories of our girlhood, pretending to be the pirates Anne Bonny and Mary Read, or the tragic princess Caroline, still filled me with longing. But the Fitzroys' finances had flourished where ours had declined, and I took no pleasure in the prospect of marriage. A season with Diana promised only embarrassing shortfalls and uncomfortable encounters.

I wanted to say all these things, and that I had seen far worse than a wounded bird in my life, for had I not seen my own mother die in childbirth? But such was not the speech of a dutiful daughter, and I quailed at the thought of disrupting our affectionate relationship. I was still struggling for words when he kissed me on my forehead and shooed me back inside, as if I was still a little girl.

I anticipated some return to the subject of laundry when my father came home, and I took care to soothe my reddened hands well before his return. But his disapproval never arrived. The Theophilus Daniels who returned was gaily whistling and positively beamed at the sight of me, despite the fact that I was helping Mrs. Simmons set the table for dinner.

"You will never guess where I have been," he declared, sitting on a stair riser and wrestling off his muddy boots.

"You were at Uncle Stuart's, sampling his port," I said, laughing, as I bent to help him. So close had we been with the Fitzroys' in my childhood, that I had taken to calling Mr. Fitzroy "Uncle," and Diana referred to my father as the same.

"Indeed I was," my father said, smiling like a little boy. "But I was not the only one! He had another visitor." He held out his fingers, as if ticking off a list. "A business acquaintance, staying in the village. Older than you, but quite worldly and prosperous. Looking for an estate to let, where he can bring friends for the weekend." His smile broadened. "Such conversation! Such carriage, such refinement! I tell you, Caroline, I have not met such a true gentleman since we were in town last season. Did I mention his business? He runs a most successful trading company. The stories he had, some of the places he's been! I could have listened to him all evening."

"And what, pray tell, is this magical man's name?" I asked, helping him up from the stairs.

"Pardon?" He blinked at me, as if brought up short by the question, and then burst out laughing. "Oh my, I didn't even say, did I? His name, my dear, is Sir Edward Masterson."

CHAPTER II

The Arrivals

*O*ver the next few weeks my father went to the village or the Fitzroys' almost every day, and each time returned with some new information regarding Sir Edward. Now we learned he had a younger brother with his own shipping company; now we learned that not only was Sir Edward keen to take up residence on our coast, he was intent on letting Harkworth Hall, a sprawling estate that had been empty for years.

Situated at the farthest end of the bay, the Hall had an uneasy history, having been built a century ago by the Harkworth family, who had subsequently fled to France under threat of death. What crime they had committed, no one knew: the most popular stories ranged from smuggling to sedition. In my own lifetime, a kindly gentleman named Archer had leased the Hall and installed his wife and young children there. For a few years, it had been the center of summer life for every well-to-do family in the county. Many of my early memories were of playing games on its grounds, and sharing in the Archers' lavish picnics ... until I had wandered into a tunnel that ran from the kitchen to a folly in the gardens, a spot so enclosed in greenery, I had believed myself utterly lost. My fright put an end to our summertime visiting. That fall, my mother and infant brother both died, and the following spring our section of the bay collapsed from the heavy rains, turning our gently sloping coastline into a useless cliff-face and destroying our pier in the process. My father withdrew for a time, and when he could finally bear to renew his acquaintanceships, the Archers had quit Harkworth Hall, declaring it too remote for their liking. Since then, it had stood empty, its surrounding copses mere smudges on the horizon, one of many memories my father and I never discussed.

Until now, it seemed. Suddenly Harkworth Hall was a topic again, as my father mused on its condition, its land, and what it might become in the right hands. I was both startled by his newfound interest in the property and curious to meet the man who had kindled that interest. But I could not bring myself to rush off to the village, to join in the gawking and parade myself before this Sir Edward—or worse still, to visit the Fitzroys and find a rival in Diana, when I longed instead for the intimacy of our youth. To find myself battling her for the attention of a stranger, competing in fashion and flirtation—no amount of curiosity could make me embrace that prospect.

Thus, I gently refused all my father's invitations and congratulated myself on my restraint. But my father can be wily when he chooses, and he was determined that if Mohammed wouldn't go to the mountain, he would bring the mountain to Mohammed.

One afternoon, I heard a vehicle in our drive, though my

father had walked to the village. The Simmonses came to me in quiet alarm: a plain black carriage was coming towards our house, who could it be? It was with wild thoughts of surgeons and injuries that we rushed to the front door, myself still in my apron from dusting the library.

When the carriage came into our drive, it halted abruptly. I did not recognize the driver, a surly-looking man who barely touched his hat. To my relief, the first person to emerge was my father, his face ruddy with ale and his expression beaming. I could not remember the last time I had seen him so happy. He came to me and took my hands in his.

"Caroline," he said solemnly, "we have a guest."

I looked over his shoulder. Disembarking from the carriage was a slight young man, his suit plain but well-tailored, his handsome profile framed by thick, dark hair bound in its ribbon. A youthful, kind face—surely he could not have achieved so much at such a young age?

And then a third man emerged from the carriage and at once my blood ran cold. My father cleared his throat and I quickly looked away, trying desperately to maintain a calm appearance.

"May I present," my father said formally, "Sir Edward Masterson and his secretary, Mister Jonathan Chase."

I found myself dropping into an awkward curtsey, simply to gain another moment to rally myself. When I pulled myself upright I found myself face-to-face with Sir Edward.

He was everything my father had claimed for him: a most handsome man, unusually tall and broad, and more handsome for his age. His suit was expensive, his wig fashionable, his sword just ornate enough, his cravat plain but of a glaring whiteness. His face was marked by the slight hauteur of the truly wealthy and his eyes were as appraising as his smile polite. In short, he was a gentleman.

Yet, from the moment I saw him disembark I felt an instinctive revulsion, and my whole body trembled with foreboding. His slightest movement only increased my fear; I was as terrified as if he had been a rabid dog. When he took my hand, it took every ounce of self-control I possessed to keep from snatching it away, or screaming, or both.

"Miss Daniels," he said in a deep voice. "Your father praised you as exemplary, yet now I find he fell far short of the mark."

"Sir Edward," I murmured in response. He bowed and kissed my hand and it was as if his lips were ice, so nerveless did that appendage become. When he stood again his eyes ran over me, pausing at my dusty apron. "Welcome to our home," I managed to add, though the word *welcome* seemed freighted with an unspoken meaning, as if I were admitting something more than a mere guest.

"Miss Daniels," Mr. Chase said, coming up the steps behind Sir Edward. "We apologize for the imposition, only the inn's comforts were few and the promise of your father's company too delightful to refuse."

I turned to him with relief, only to find myself discombobulated again: here, too, there was something odd, though he did not provoke the fear that his employer did. He bowed deeply, then took my hand and kissed it, his lips just brushing my knuckles. As he straightened, he reached inside his coat and tugged at his clothes, just under his arm. The gesture seemed odd yet familiar, but I could not think on why as my father was speaking.

"Sir Edward has agreed to stay with us while the Hark-worth Hall lease is finalized." He put an arm around my waist, and I found myself pressing close to him. "Won't it be marvelous to see the Hall opened once more? We are overdue, I think, to make new memories there."

It struck me then. The gesture of Mr. Chase was precisely that of a woman tugging on her stays. But why would a young man wear such a garment?

"And so you shall again, my friend, for I hope to be settled within the month," Sir Edward said. He turned to his secretary. "We are still on schedule, yes?"

Mr. Chase nodded. "I am meeting with the lawyer in the morning, and if all are amenable then we will proceed with haste." As he spoke, his gaze met mine and I fancied I saw something sly in his eyes, as if we shared a secret. Could it be? It was ludicrous to even think it—what a scandal if she were discovered! Traveling with an unmarried man, walking about in nothing but breeches. In town, I had seen actresses go about dressed as men—but what honorable gentleman would have an actress for a companion? It was far more likely that he had some illness or malformation that required the garment.

"Marvelous," my father said. "So, you can stay for dinner?" He gave my waist a little squeeze. "I sent word to Fitzroy as we left the village, my dear, to join us. Won't it be splendid? It's been far too long since we entertained."

Behind me Mrs. Simmons gave a little squeak of fright, and I swallowed my own instinctive cry. Six for dinner, with no notice? And what if there was something improper about Mr. Chase?

"That's very kind of you," Sir Edward said, looking at Mr. Chase. "But I believe we have other matters that must be seen to besides the lease—"

"Certainly, I cannot stay late," Mr. Chase put in. His voice was soft, almost lilting, yet no one seemed to notice. "But a good dinner would allow me an early start in the morning."

I had always prided myself on a robust constitution. I could walk all the way to the village, I rode well, I had insisted on being taught to shoot to help provide game. I could dress meat and muck out the stalls as well as Mr. Simmons himself. Yet now I felt decidedly faint. We were to entertain this strange, possibly scandalous, pair, with Diana and her father as witnesses, and all on a few pigeons and a bowlful of vegetables—

"Then it's decided," my father declared. "Simmons, help the coachman please. Let us all go into the drawing room for some refreshment."

I made myself smile, smile as if my life depended on it, and stepped aside to let my father and Sir Edward precede me into the house. As he followed, Mr. Chase seemed about to address me, but I quickly curtseyed again and he passed without speaking. His movements were so lithe, so easy— oh, if the impossible were true and he truly was a woman? She would be my girlhood games come to life, the very incarnation of the etching of Mary Read I had pored over in my youth: trousered, hair down, striding boldly through the world.

Slowly I returned to the house, shutting the doors behind me. Already the men were talking boisterously in the drawing room. Sir Edward laughed, loud and braying, and it seemed as if the hall grew darker in response, as if he were smothering the sun itself with his bellowing. Beneath my apron, my hand still burned with cold where his lips had touched my skin. It was with relief that I saw Mrs. Simmons beckoning to me from the end of the hall, her face creased with worry. I hurried to her side. It would take all our cleverness to wring a proper dinner from our paltry larder. I could not say where Mr. Chase had gone to and I did not care to know.

CHAPTER III

The Dinner-Party

Dinner was nothing short of a miracle. The soup was so thin as to be water and the wines mismatched from our dwindling cellar; yet somehow Mr. Simmons managed to produce a smoked ham, half a bushel of vegetables, two crisp loaves, and Emily, their niece who lived in the village and worked at the inn. How he did this while also settling Sir Edward and stabling the horses, I had no idea. I had gone upstairs to change my clothes, only to find myself overwhelmed by the intricacies of my wardrobe, for I had not dressed properly for dinner since we were last in town months ago. Completely at a loss, I went back to the kitchen to see if I could help further—only to find Emily bustling about, a pie in the oven, and the potatoes boiling. Mrs. Simmons shooed me back to my room with an offer to send Emily to lace me once the remaining vegetables were chopped.

I was therefore left to the operation of dressing for dinner. My powder was caked from winter damp, my hoops smelled faintly of mildew, and I did not have a pair of stockings that could be called white with any honesty. Still I managed to come up with a not-embarrassing combination of dress and petticoats—though the former could have used a good pressing—but that was what candlelight was for: masking my numerous flaws.

I was half-dressed and waiting on Emily when the door opened. I turned to reprimand her for her presumption and instead spread my arms wide as Diana Fitzroy came into the room. What a welcome sight she was! She smelled of lilacs and the fresh air from the ride, her pale face was radiant, perfectly framed by her upswept, powdered hair; her embrace as comforting as my mother's had been. I suddenly found myself dangerously close to tears, and when we drew apart her keen eyes spotted the gleam in my own.

"Darling! Whatever is the matter?" She sat me down upon my bed and dabbed at my eyes with her handkerchief. "Is he really that marvelous? Remember, dear Caroline, you have a good head on your shoulders—that's quite the prize for a merchant."

I stared at her. "Whatever do you mean?"

"Why, Sir Edward, of course!" She sat down beside me, laughing gaily. "It's the talk of the village that he's chosen to stay with you, you know."

"Oh." In my worries over my clothes and the food, I had forgotten just who I was dressing for. The coldness, the way the house had seemed to darken …

"You don't seem very excited." She angled her head, trying to catch my gaze. "Caroline, what is it? I've met the gentleman several times now, he's perfectly splendid. They say—pure gossip, mind you—but they say he has close to two thousand a year. Two thousand! Think of it! He could probably buy Harkworth Hall if he liked, or anywhere that suited you."

At that I laughed. To find myself mistress of such an estate—it was absurd. "You speak as if we're already engaged," I said. "We have seen each other for all of a few minutes, and spoken half a dozen words."

Diana merely laid a finger on the side of her nose, then twirled it about. "Let me lace you," she said.

Obediently I rose and turned. She pulled the laces hard, harder than Mrs. Simmons, but when I asked her to loosen them she shook her head.

"You are far too lax with your appearance," she chided, knotting the laces firmly. "This is serious, Caroline. I think he is a very good match for you. You will be doing both yourself and your father a disservice to not present yourself in the best possible light."

At the mention of my father, I blushed. She was right, of course. Two thousand pounds would keep us both splendidly—I owed it to him to give Sir Edward every consideration.

She helped me into my dress then set about pinning my stomacher, though I told her I could as easily do so. Her hands against my belly, sliding up and down as she smoothed the fabric into place—there was a gentleness, a tenderness, in her touch that I had not felt since I was a child. My breath was catching a little, in all likelihood from the tight corset, but she glanced up at me and I saw her cheeks were pink.

"When we are both married," she said in a low voice, "we will, of course, have to visit each other often. It would be almost like when we were younger, do you remember?"

I could only nod. I dared not speak.

"Sometimes I miss those days," she said, turning her attention back to the pins.

She had artfully swept up her hair and dotted it with little jewels. It left her nape wonderfully bare. I suddenly wanted to embrace her, to press my face to her neck and never, ever let her go.

"There." She stood abruptly, turning me one way and another. "Nearly presentable," she said. Pointing at my mirror, she gave me a hug and a kiss on the cheek. "Though what we can do about that face I'm not quite sure. You look as if you're about to be bled, not dine with a charming man."

I forced the corners of my mouth to curve upwards. It looked nothing like a smile to me, more the grimace of a death-mask, but Diana nodded in approval. "That's my girl," she declared. "That's how we win."

I kept the smile on my face as we did my hair and make-up, and as she dropped to her knees to fit my shoes. As little girls, the story of Anne and Mary had captured my imagination, but Diana preferred to play royalty. It had involved being dressed in just this manner, though our games had neglected to include the sick feeling in my belly, or the cold sweat that was trickling beneath my arms. Diana tutted at the state of my powder but managed to coax out enough to smooth my sun-darkened cheeks. Only then was I permitted to leave my room.

But oh! It was worth it to see my father's face. It lit up as I had not seen it in some time. He could not have been prouder if it had indeed been my wedding day. He beamed as he escorted me into the dining room, followed by Diana on Sir Edward's arm, and Uncle Stuart with Mr. Chase. The latter, I noticed, had changed into an evening suit. He easily responded to the address of Mister, and again I marveled that no one else seemed to question his presentation—no one, that is, save Diana. I caught her giving Mr. Chase a thorough examination and her sweet bow of a lip decidedly curled. I was not the only one who sensed something different in our guest.

And yet. The ease with which he walked to his seat and claimed it, the way he conversed so freely with the men—it made something clench inside me. If my instinct was correct, how could any woman behave so, without fear of censure? When Uncle Stuart expounded upon the state of trade, he responded easily with financial reports from London. When the wine was poured, he remarked upon its provenance and his travels in Italy, and the men all made noises of agreement. Meanwhile Diana and I simply ate, and smiled. When I met Diana's gaze she gave me little nods. In her eyes, it seemed, everything was going well. Yet, I felt a sudden, overwhelming longing to be able to speak as Mr. Chase did—and to have had the worldly experiences that lay behind such conversation. I had only been to London once, and much of England was as unknown to me as our sister countries on the Continent.

My father and Uncle Stuart sat at either end of the table. I had been seated at my father's right, and Sir Edward sat across from me. Mr. Chase was beside me, across from Diana. The proximity afforded me a closer inspection. I noted with increasing certainty the smoothness of his cheek, the height of his cravat which concealed his throat. That Diana avoided looking directly at Mr. Chase was obvious, and Mr. Chase turned slightly, so as to direct his remarks towards my father and Sir Edward.

"I was wondering, Mister Daniels," he said, "if you have any knowledge of the tunnels that run beneath the Hall. They were omitted from the property description, yet apparently they are common knowledge—as are the criminal activities that provoked their creation."

It was then that I saw it. Sir Edward, who, until now, had been subdued in his manner, seemed to almost swell in his seat, his brow darkening as he looked at Mr. Chase, though he said nothing.

"I suspect the reason they were not mentioned is because they have either collapsed, or are in danger of doing so," Uncle Stuart remarked. "The Harkworths made their fortune running goods in from the bay—and more than a few seditionists, if there's any truth to rumor. But those tunnels are nearly a century old now. Last family that lived there sealed all the doors that led to them. Damn things could kill you."

"Father," Diana said reprovingly.

"Come, Fitzroy, that's not completely true," my father said. "The Archers used at least one to get to the stables when it rained, and you remember when Caroline ran off down another."

All gazes turned to me; I found myself blushing. "I was but a child," I demurred. "And it only went to the gardens. Hardly useful for committing crimes."

"Though quite useful for an assignation," Diana tittered.

Her remark only deepened my blush. I could not look at Sir Edward.

"The one that ran to the bay is still standing," my father put in, seemingly oblivious to Diana's meaning. "At least, you can still see the opening. It's just a shadow in the cliffs, but it's there, all right. You can even see part of the beam they used to winch up their contraband. I've heard that it followed what was once an underground stream. Maybe that's why it held up longer than the others."

There was an awkward pause. I was trying to think of a new topic of conversation when Sir Edward suddenly spoke.

"It is entirely possible that this coastline is laced with underground waterways," he said in a low voice. "Many do not realize just how much water lies within England's green lands. They are the bedrock of English power, the very veins through which her lifeblood runs. We would do well to treat them with the respect—nay, the *reverence*—they deserve."

His voice caused a hush to fall over the room. It seemed larger than the man himself; it seemed to come from both without and somehow within, as if he were echoed by a voice in my mind.

"We first settled close to water because we knew its strength and power. Even now, our greatest cities are those clinging to the edges of rivers or seas, drawing sustenance from the water lapping at their borders. Our might in trade and conquest derives from this holiest of sources, and those who have devoted themselves to understanding its energies and its needs."

He rose and held his wine glass, half-full, over the center of the table. In the candlelight, it seemed to contain patterns on its surface. I could not stop gazing upon it. Indeed, I felt myself leaning forward to see more clearly, and sensed the others do the same.

"From the mightiest ocean to the smallest tributary, all are ours by the grace of God," Sir Edward continued, his voice low and melodic, almost as if he were singing. "Water is ours to master, ours to wield. But like any beast, we must treat it properly. We must care for it, and discipline it, or it will consume us."

Upon the blood-red surface rose the shimmering outline of England and the roiling waters around it. As he spoke, the crimson sea churned and foamed, the waves crashing high upon the cliffs—

—and then the sea seemed to part, as if pressed apart by invisible hands, and there was something in its depths, something coiling and serpentine that rose up in a mass of undulating limbs and seized the whole of the island to itself—

—and then England was gone, drawn down into the wine with an audible splash.

At once the wine was merely wine again. The candles seemed to brighten, though I did not remember them dimming.

"Well said," said my father. "Well said, indeed."

I heard a tremor in his voice that matched my own trembling. I felt faint and sick; I felt distinctly unclean. To distract myself, I looked to our other guests. Diana and Uncle Stuart seemed excited, as if witnesses to a thrilling bit of theater, but Mr. Chase looked as ill as I felt. His hand was coiling and uncoiling on the table, making a white-knuckled fist and relaxing. When he caught my gaze, he quickly moved it to his lap.

"That you think it merely a speech saddens me, my dear Daniels," Sir Edward said calmly. "We have grown far from our true nature indeed, if we cannot comprehend the very thing that sustains us."

"I think we are well aware of our power," Uncle Stuart declared. "Only the French dare challenge us now, and the last time they tried, they couldn't even get across the Channel. Now I hear they are melting the silver in Versailles to pay their debts. They lack both the money and the discipline to ever truly threaten us."

"I would not be so quick to dismiss them," Sir Edward said. "They seek to spread their influence as much as we do. Even now, in Paris they talk of war. Never before has England been so poised for conquest. It means we must act with even greater vigilance to maintain our advantage, lest we lose all."

"Preposterous. It is only a matter of time before we crush the French utterly. As you say, we have the power—"

"Father!" Diana gave him a pointed look. "We are a mixed company. Surely we can choose a topic of conversation that includes us all?"

"I would like to hear more about this power," I blurted out.

I cannot say what possessed me to speak so, and I was given no opportunity to reflect on it, for something struck me in the shin, so hard I nearly cried out. Beside me, Mr. Chase said smoothly, "I believe, Miss Daniels, that Sir Edward is speaking in loose metaphors." When I turned to him, both astonished and outraged, I found him gazing at Sir Edward with a grim expression. "*We*, of course, are the true power of England. All this talk of water is a metaphor for her people, and their skills and courage. That is what he speaks of."

Sir Edward returned Mr. Chase's grim expression; and then his own softened, and a pall that had covered the room lifted.

"Mister Chase's explanation is crude, but correct in its essence," he said. "I only speak so to stress to everyone the importance of our united front. We are beset as we never have been before, even as we build an empire the likes of which the world has never seen."

"To England," my father cried, with a startling fervor.

"To England," Mr. Chase echoed. Now he looked at me, and his meaning was as clear as if he had spoken it aloud: *do not press this.*

Unwillingly I raised my glass with the others. We toasted our country, my shin still throbbing, and then were saved from further conversation by the arrival of the second course, including a commendable pigeon pie. But I was certain now, absolutely certain, that Sir Edward was not here to woo me at all, nor to deepen his friendship with my father. Something else had brought him to this county, and our door.

"He is marvelous," Diana said as she dealt the cards between us. Her gaze had not left the half-open door to the dining room. "Such vision! Such passion! It is a far cry from the young men who think only of gambling and horses."

"You did not think it strange?" I asked, keeping my voice low. "How he spoke—it felt almost like a dream, like when you feel awake but are still sleeping ..." I trailed off, trying to find the words.

"That is not strange, Caroline," Diana whispered, smiling. "That's infatuation." She glanced at the dining room again. "Though I do not like his companion."

I followed her gaze. Mr. Chase had stepped in front of the open doorway. He looked over his shoulder at us, and then turned completely.

"It is indecent to keep someone so ... effeminate, in such close capacity," Diana whispered as Mr. Chase crossed the hall. "I have hinted as much these past days. You would do well to make it known that you will not tolerate such a presence in your household."

I could not reply to this as Mr. Chase was upon us. "I wanted to thank you, Miss Daniels, for your hospitality," he said. "Sadly, I must depart. I need to make an early start in the morning, so it's best if I leave from the village."

"An admirable plan," Diana said curtly.

Her tone startled me. Though she had never been above gossip, she had always behaved charmingly in public. That she was blatantly displaying her dislike for Mr. Chase was a first.

"I do hope you will find the journey amenable," I said. "The road to the village is not the best, and it is treacherous after dark if you are not familiar with its defects. Perhaps Mister Simmons can accompany you?"

"He has, in fact, already offered that service," Mr. Chase

replied. "But I think it best if he stay here, to settle Sir Edward. Our coachman is a canny driver, he has guided us through worse."

"I see." I tried not to blush. I caught well his delicacy regarding our staff, and the foolishness of my offer. Send Mr. Simmons out now and there would be no one to see to either my father or Sir Edward, and what would the latter think of us?

Still, Mr. Chase lingered at the doorway, watching me with an expression I could not comprehend. Diana cleared her throat; when I looked at her she angled her head, then mouthed, *The door*. At once I blushed properly—of course! Mrs. Simmons was cleaning up, Mr. Simmons was waiting on the men.

"I will show you out," I said with as much dignity as I could muster. I rose from the chair, forgetting the volume of my skirts, and nearly knocked it over. Quickly, Mr. Chase hurried to my side and pulled away the inconvenient furniture. "Thank you," I added, ignoring my burning face, and led the way to the hall.

It was a few short steps to the doors and I crossed them as swiftly as decency permitted. I was suddenly overcome by a strange, nervous exhaustion, more wounded animal than tired hostess. First the strange display at dinner, then here I was stumbling about, having to be prompted to common courtesy. That my failing should be witnessed by the likes of Mr. Chase only made it more painful. I wanted him to know, somehow, how unsettled he made me. I wanted him to know that if he was, indeed, a woman, anyone would

look at his relation to Sir Edward and assume the worst. I
wanted him to know that none of us could simply behave as
we pleased, no matter how we might long to.

It was with relief that we arrived at the door, but when
I reached for the knob he laid a hand over it first. "Miss
Daniels," he began in a low voice. "I know you do not know
me, and I know, too, you have divined I am not quite as I
appear. Nevertheless, I must speak with you."

And there it was: my instinct proved correct, yet it only
unnerved me further. "We are not in London, *Miss* Chase,"
I said as coolly as I could manage. "Forgive us our lack of
fashion. We are too simple for such radical practices."

But she was waving her hand, as if to shoo my words
away. "I am appealing not to your fashion but your sense,"
she said. "I beg of you, do not rush into any decisions regarding Sir Edward. He is not what you think him."

"Pardon?" I demanded. "If you think I have, I have *designs*
on your—on him—" I could not even find the words. All
the possible permutations of their debauchery rose before me.

Again she waved her hand at me. "I care nothing for your
designs!" she hissed. "But you must demand accounts from
him. Demand proofs of his businesses, his character. And
for God's sake, do not go anywhere alone with him." She
took a breath, clearly struggling for words. "Especially not to
the sea …"

Footsteps made us both look up. Sir Edward stood in the
hallway. "Leaving, Chase?" he said.

"Indeed, sir." Miss Chase smiled, as easily as if we had
been discussing the weather. "I was just taking my leave of

Miss Daniels."

"I wish you a safe and pleasant journey," I said pointedly, and opened the door without so much as a curtsey. The cool night air was a welcome balm, blowing away much of my agitation.

"Miss Daniels." She took my hand in a dramatic bow and kissed it. A kiss that lingered a beat too long, that felt her thumb slide along my palm—or did I imagine it? Certainly, she seemed unchanged when she arose, but oh! My hand burned, it burned, with a sensation I had never felt before. It was everything that Sir Edward's kiss was not, it set every nerve alight in my body.

"Ask him about his wives," she whispered. And with a curt nod to Sir Edward, she was gone.

CHAPTER IV

A Secret Revealed

$\mathcal{I}$t was some time later when Diana and Uncle Stuart took their leave. Diana's hands in mine, the encouraging kiss on my cheek and her sly look at Sir Edward … I wanted both to pull her to me and to never see anyone ever again, so great was my exhaustion.

Once they had departed, Sir Edward announced he would retire, and Mr. Simmons hurried ahead of him to ready his bedroom. Leaving my father to tidy the dining room, I went to the kitchen to see if I could provide Mrs. Simmons with any belated help.

The kitchen, however, was in an excellent state. Mrs. Simmons and Emily were putting away the last of the foodstuffs, neither looking too tired for the effort. Yet, I was struck again by the quantity of food, and I dropped helplessly into a chair while Mrs. Simmons clucked about dirtying my dress and Emily fixed me with a rapturous smile.

"We cannot afford this," I cried, gesturing to the remains. "How will we repay so much on credit?"

"Never fear, Miss, it wasn't all on credit." Mrs. Simmons wiped her hands before patting my shoulder. "That Mister Chase did much of the arranging. He told Mister Simmons it was the least they could do, for imposing so suddenly. He even paid for Emily."

"Mam wouldn't have let me go for free, not with the baby due," Emily confirmed, tossing back her plait of reddish-brown hair. "Though I think it was Sir Edward's idea. Oh, Miss, he's ever so wonderful! So handsome, and so full of—" She cried out as Mrs. Simmons swatted her and went back to her wiping with a scowl.

I could not speak for my surprise, which at once turned to anguish. First I make a fool of myself, then all her strange warnings, and now I was indebted to her. I tried to tot up the full cost of the night, but my mind could not make the numbers come. I kept coming back to the humiliation and weariness I felt, and what was the cost of that?

"Let me undo those knots," Mrs. Simmons said, helping me up, "and then you get yourself to bed, Miss. You look done in."

She turned me like a child and unknotted my laces. The rush of air was so powerful I felt light-headed. Had I been so close to fainting all night? Perhaps that accounted for the strange power of Sir Edward's presentation ...

But no, no, there had been something about it, something *awful*.

"Miss," Emily said in a smaller voice, "if you're looking for staff at the Hall ... I mean, after you're married and all ..."

And though nothing had been decided, indeed nothing had even begun, I felt a sudden, absolute certainty: no matter what, I would never be mistress of that place; to envision such a thing was to see only darkness ahead.

Ask him about his wives.

"That's enough, Emily." Mrs. Simmons took me by the elbow and steered me to the kitchen door. "Go to bed, Miss," she said more kindly. "Everything will be more sensible in the morning."

That night I dreamed that I walked down to our little stretch of coast, save that everything was wine-red, sea and sky and land all the same crimson hue. Before me, the waters parted to reveal a deep chasm, and in its depths something pulsed obscenely. I leaned over, trying to see, and just as the pulsing mass split open to reveal a single staring eye, I was falling, falling …

… only to awaken in the darkness with my heart racing and my shift damp with sweat. Silently, I prayed that something would simply make Sir Edward vanish, would remove him and his secretary utterly from our lives. Only then was I able to lie back and finally fall into an empty, restless sleep.

CHAPTER V

Three Unpleasant Stories

The next morning, I had to struggle to get out of bed. My mind felt thick, though I had drunk little the night before. More difficult, however, was a general unwillingness to leave the peaceful nest of my bedroom. I dreaded greeting our guest; I dreaded the conversation we might engage in over breakfast. His presence in the house was almost palpable, even through the walls, seeming to cast a pall on everything despite the patchy sunlight that revealed itself when I opened the shutters.

Just then, I saw Sir Edward's large frame appear below my window. I instinctively ducked behind the drapes, peeking out at him. He did not look up; instead he strode unerringly in the direction of our coastline. His heavy, black overcoat flapped open as he walked, making him appear like a swooping bird coming low over its prey.

Only then did I realize that the birds had not returned since the day my father had met Sir Edward. Nothing, not even a wolf, could have so utterly frightened them.

Nothing, perhaps, save that creature in the water.

But even as I thought this, I chided myself for my foolishness. It was one thing to dislike the man, another entirely to start imagining such ridiculous things. No wonder I was hiding in my bedroom like a child. My father approved of him, as did the Fitzroys; even Emily seemed smitten with him. Yet here I was envisioning monsters.

Still, it was a relief to come downstairs and find only my father at the table, buried in his newspaper. A small pile of unopened envelopes sat by his plate—all bills, presumably—and I thought again of last night. How much did we owe Miss Chase, and how would we ever repay her? Because repay her we must. The mere thought of leaving such a debt between us, no matter the reasoning behind her generosity, made me feel sick as little else did. That woman! I glanced at my poor father. How would he feel to know he had spoken so freely with a woman, and one in breeches, no less? I found myself blushing for him, and instead focused on assembling my own plate. It was only then that I noticed I, too, had a letter.

The elegant handwriting was unknown to me, but there were few who had cause to write me. When I thought through the possibilities, I felt faint. Would he address himself to me after one evening? Was it merely a first shot across the bows? For the first time, I wished I had paid more attention to Diana's natterings, that I would have some comprehension of how these matters usually advanced. I glanced at my father again as I picked up the envelope, but he seemed engrossed in his paper, without so much as a peek in my direction. His ignorance made me relax slightly. Whatever it was, it couldn't be an offer.

I opened it carefully, noting the plain seal, but inside found nothing save three small, yellowed clippings. As I read them over, my nervousness became outright fear, then horror. For each clipping described the death—the *violent* death—of a newly married woman. Each woman had been robbed, and her throat cut; each had subsequently been thrown into a body of water. I felt nerveless. Inadvertently I looked to the wall, in the direction that Sir Edward had taken, where I knew the waves churned endlessly against our shore.

Ask him about his wives.

"Gone to meet his maker."

I jumped at my father's voice, the clippings falling from my hand.

"Funny, that," my father went on, not looking up. "That was the note I got this morning. 'Gone to meet my maker. Back later this morning.' Simmons saw him leave this morning, said he was taking a walk to see the water. And here I was starting to think the fellow had no sense of humor." He finally looked up, his brow furrowing. "Caroline? Are you ill, child? You're as pale as death."

"I—I don't feel well," I managed, fitting the clippings back into the envelope. My hands were shaking. In my mind, I was walking by the water's edge. Hands would seize me, and that terrible searing pain across my throat …

My father rang for Mrs. Simmons, who hurried to my side, clucking about my exhaustion and the strain of managing a party. She helped me out of the chair, assuring my father that all I needed was to go back to bed and rest.

Halfway up the stairs, however, she whispered, "He's not gone and pulled a fast one, has he?"

"Pardon?" I looked at her, utterly bewildered, my mind still whirling with horrors.

"That Mister Chase. Mister Simmons thought the note was from him—he's not left you with all those bills, or—"

"Oh! No, it was not that at all." I struggled to form a sensible reply. "I think it is just as you said. It was such a strain yesterday, and I slept poorly."

"And then you got right up, thinking to be there for your guest, when he was off this morning with barely a word." She clucked again as she shut my bedroom door behind us. "He's a handsome enough gentleman, but he's got a strange way about him, and that secretary of his is downright queer. Don't get me wrong, he was more than a help last night, but there's something about him." She shook her head as she helped me undress. "They raise them funny down in London, that's for sure."

I heard her words, and yet they seemed to come from a great distance. My throat ached, but it was only when Mrs. Simmons guided me into bed that I realized I had been rubbing my hand beneath my jaw, over and over, right where I imagined the cut would come. In my other hand, I still clutched the envelope. I put it on the nightstand.

"You just rest, Miss," Mrs. Simmons said, fluffing the pillows behind me. "I'll bring you something light in a little while. Proper rest is what you need."

As soon as she shut the door, however, I was on my feet again. I went to the window, then to the door, as if I could somehow flee everything. I was safe for the moment in my room, but for how long? And what of my father, and the

Simmonses? What of Diana? If I were out of reach, would he set his sights on her?

At last, I managed to calm myself enough to sit down on the edge of the bed and open the envelope once more. Miss Chase's warning had implied that Sir Edward was perhaps a rake—not an unusual specimen even in our remote corner of the world. But these clippings—! I could not believe them, and yet it seemed that she, at least, thought them to be true. But what person, man or woman, could work for such a monster? Unless she sought to besmirch his character and repulse me utterly—but then why go to such lengths, why find such gruesome material? If there were any truth to them, then her employer was for the gallows, and perhaps herself as well.

If there were any truth to them …

I studied them more thoroughly, tucking myself back into the safety of my eiderdown before I focused on the grisly paragraphs. The women had all been new brides; in each case the husband had to be sent for, which meant he had been away—or at least, had pretended to be away so as to escape culpability. In one, the woman had been the daughter of a peer, so the article was longer, describing her recent wedding to "a prosperous merchant, newly arrived," and the family property they had moved into.

An estate by the sea, with its own stretch of coastline.

That there were similarities between us could not be denied. Yet in each case I could see no motive other than money, and what did I have to offer in that regard? Surely Sir Edward knew of our approximate circumstances, if not every detail—my father struggled to hold his tongue at the best of times, and a few pints would have brought out the picture in sum.

It was then that I heard my father's voice outside, calling to someone. I hurried to the window and watched as he walked towards the waiting Sir Edward, pulling on his coat and hat as he did so. He had forgotten his sword, I saw with a pang. For a moment, I felt a cold dread that they would go back to the coast, but instead they began walking down the road to the village.

Still I could not rest. I would have given much to put questions to Miss Chase at that moment—hard questions. If there were anything that connected Sir Edward to these crimes, why was it that she had not gone to the constabulary? Did she think to scare me off? Or perhaps she thought I would go to the constabulary myself, only to be made a fool for such an absurd accusation.

These were not the limit of my options, however. One of the clippings mentioned both the name of the victim and the village she had resided in, which was fairly close to our own. Surely there must be a relation who could speak for her. Though I did not know how long ago all these deaths were—only one showed the year, seven years ago now; the one close by had no date at all.

I sat down at my desk and wrote swiftly, barely letting myself think. An inquiry, nothing more. Just an inquiry. *Demand proofs*, Miss Chase had said. Well, I would do just that, though perhaps not in a way she anticipated. Considering the circumstances, I could hardly expect either herself or

Sir Edward to be honest, but a relation of this poor woman might be eager to speak.

I wrote it out a second time, cleanly, and threw the first into the fire. I sealed the envelope and addressed it to the lady's family. With that task completed, I felt I could finally rest, if for no other reason than to rally my strength for what lay ahead.

CHAPTER VI

Poetry

*L*ater that day, when Mrs. Simmons brought up my tea, I asked her carefully, "If a stranger warned you that you were about to, ah … embark on a bad financial scheme, would you listen to them?"

"Listen, yes," she said as she settled the tray on my lap. "But heed? The question I would ask is what do they stand to gain from it?"

My life, I nearly replied, but instead I nodded.

"Your father's not about to do anything rash, is he?" she asked, looking at me searchingly.

"Hmm? Oh no, no." I started to wolf down my food, only to remember I was supposed to be ill. I was in no hurry to resume my duties caring for our guest. "Are they well, the gentlemen?"

"I believe so. They returned a few minutes ago, and now Sir Edward has your father pulling out all sorts of papers." She frowned at me. "Miss, if there's something Mister Simmons and I should know—"

"What kind of papers?" I interrupted.

"Well, funnily enough, it's mostly maps. I think your father is trying to show him where the pier used to be." She sighed and shifted my drapes, filtering the grey afternoon light. "Do you remember much of that time, Miss? It was so different then."

At once the memory of my mother filled me, so strong, so overwhelming, as to be almost palpable. "Yes," I whispered. "Yes, I remember."

"To everything there is a season," Mrs. Simmons said piously. But she stopped at my bed and kissed my cap before she left the room, as she had not done since those first lonely years after my mother passed.

I had no time to dwell on the gesture, however, for no sooner had she left there was a knock on my door and my father peeked in on me. When he saw me sitting upright and taking tea, he smiled. I foolishly smiled back and beckoned him in, only to feel my smile vanish when Sir Edward appeared behind him.

After my wild imaginings and glimpses, though, he seemed far less intimidating. His smile was kind, his presence appropriately reticent for all that my father ushered him in. He seemed to have lost the looming, commanding aura from the previous evening. It seemed impossible that this man could be the same one who had conjured such frightful visions at our table, much less be guilty of far greater villainy.

My father gestured him to the chair by my bed and took for himself my desk chair. "You are looking much better," he said, his voice a little loud. "I've been ever so worried, and then Sir Edward suggested that we could visit with you and see for ourselves."

"Your father was ready to send for a physician," Sir Edward put in. "But I told him that no full-blooded Englishwoman would be so undone by a mere dinner party. Tired, certainly, but not truly ill." Before I could reply to this odd sentiment, he held up a book. "We thought perhaps we might read to you?"

"Oh! Certainly," I said, settling into my pillows. With my father in the room, it would be an innocuous way to pass an afternoon—and then they would go to dinner, and that would be one day done with. Tomorrow I could perhaps extend my illness, and thereafter a reply to my letter might come … thought what might happen then, I didn't want to think on.

My father patted my hand and made himself comfortable in the chair. From beneath his arm, Sir Edward produced a worn, anonymous volume. I inclined my head in what I hoped was an attentive manner, closing my eyes. With luck, I would perhaps doze a little and they would excuse themselves appropriately.

Sir Edward cleared his voice and began to read:

Sweet rural scene!
Of flocks and green!
At careless ease my limbs are spread;
All nature still
But yonder rill;
And listening pines not o'er my head:

In prospect wide,
The boundless tide!
Waves cease to foam, and winds to roar;

Without a breeze,
The curling seas
Dance on, in measure, to the shore.

Who sings the source
Of wealth and force?
Vast field of commerce and big war:
Where wonders dwell!
Where terrors swell!
And Neptune thunders from his car?

I opened my eyes, startled, and looked at my father. He looked as startled as I felt and when he quickly averted his face, I realized he was hiding a smile. What swain, no matter his age or temperament, would read such a poem to an ill lady? The more I thought on it, the more I, too, saw the humor in it and had to bite my cheeks. My father, catching my eye, shook his head wryly and we exchanged little smiles.

The main! the main!
Is Britain's reign;
Her strength, her glory, is her fleet;
The main! the main!
Be Briton's strain;
As Triton's strong, as Syren's sweet.

Through nature wide,
Is nought descry'd
So rich in pleasure, or surprize;

When all-serene
How sweet the scene!
How dreadful, when the billows rise.

And storms deface
The fluid glass
In which ere-while Britannia fair
Look'd down with pride,
Like Ocean's bride,
Adjusting her majestic air.

Sir Edward's voice was deepening, taking on the same strange quality that it had at dinner the previous evening. I saw my father's face slacken, his eyelids droop. Alarmed, I turned my attention back to Sir Edward, only to find his gaze fixed on me, his eyes seemingly black in the afternoon shadows, his voice as formal as any priest's:

When rushes forth
The frowning North
On blackening billows, with what dread
My shuddering soul
Beholds them roll,
And hears their roarings o'er my head!

With terror mark
Yon flying bark!
Now, center-deep descend the brave;
Now, toss'd on high

It takes the sky,
A feather on the towering wave!

As he spoke, I found myself not in my room, but in my dream from the previous night: staring down, down, at the churning water as it parted, dreading what lay within its depths—

—and then there was a knock on my door, and Sir Edward's voice stopped as if his throat had been cut. My father jerked awake with a cough and shook himself. Mr. Simmons carefully opened the door, and begged our pardon, but he had found the chest of papers the gentlemen had asked for.

"Excellent," my father declared, stretching himself as if he had just awakened from a deep slumber. When he saw my expression, he added, "These are the plans your grandfather had drawn up when he first considered leasing the coast, my dear. The surveys and assessments."

"But the land has long since given way," I said. "I cannot see what interest they hold—"

"They are vastly interesting, Miss Daniels," Sir Edward said. He had risen, the little book had vanished; once more he was merely a man. "As I have explained to your father, this bay is uniquely situated for a trading scheme my brother and I are considering, one with such profits as to make refurbishing the beachfront a financially viable proposition." He nodded at my father. "Knowing what it once was, and what the soundings are close to the cliffs, will help me to assess the situation. Your neighbor Fitzroy has already shown me his surveys."

My father gestured for him to go ahead, then came and sat on the edge of my bed. "He is an unusual fellow, is he not?" he whispered. Before I could reply he held up his hand. "I know—I know he is not what you might have imagined," he continued, choosing his words with care. "I doubt you dreamed of an older gentleman who would read you such nonsense. All I ask, Caroline, is that you do not reject him before you know him. Give it a little time." He hesitated again. "You would not want, with him. You would never want for anything, and to have that certainty … it has a value of its own."

The emotion in his voice, the way his hand trembled—I felt my own tears rising. "Father," I whispered, taking his hand in mine to stop that terrible shaking. "Of course I will do as you ask. Only I do not think he is interested in me at all."

"He has asked about you," he said. "Not directly, but he has brought you up many times—asking about your poor mother, our ancestors. I think it possible that an affection may emerge, given time?" He smiled then, shyly. "And perhaps you will forgive an old man for being more keen to enter into business with a son-in-law, rather than a friend."

I could not think of how to respond. He seemed to take my silence as assent, and with a brief kiss on my cheek, left the room. I felt sick at heart. To have my father so hopeful! It overshadowed even the clippings, even the strange vision from dinner. No scenario I could conjure—even one that cast Miss Chase as Sir Edward's vengeful, debauched mistress—lessened the pain my father would experience should his friendship with Sir Edward come to naught. His hopes were so earnest, so centered on my well-being, that I felt ashamed. Here he was trying to ensure my future, and I thinking only of that strange woman and her wild accusations.

My face burned. I tried to sleep. After all, I had engineered my own confinement, I might as well take advantage of the rest. Yet, I could not quiet my mind from its swirling images: Miss Chase's grim looks; Sir Edward striding towards our coastline; those murdered, drowned bodies. My father's hope. That strange, reptilian eye that had gazed upon me.

At some point that night, I awoke to darkness with a start. I felt convinced, utterly convinced, that the room was being flooded, that we were being carried away to the sea. Everything smelled and tasted of salt; my ears were roaring, roaring. The sensations were strong enough that when I swung my feet out of bed, I expected to feel water. In a panic, I opened my door and stepped into the hall. At once, all the sensations vanished and the air smelled normal once more, filled only with the soft creaks and sighs of our house.

For the first time in my life, I locked my bedroom door.

CHAPTER VII

An Outing

The next morning, I was roused by Mrs. Simmons rattling the doorknob. She seemed disturbed even when I offered poor dreams as an explanation, and hinted darkly that she was going to renew my father's sentiments for a physician's perspective. My subterfuge had run its course. Unwillingly, I roused myself and dressed, with many reassurances as to the state of my nerves. My head felt thick from the previous night. It was a relief to open the window to the clean, briny air and breathe deeply. My best course of action, I decided, was to bear the next few days as best I could. Perhaps once Sir Edward was gone, my father's interest would wane.

I found the gentlemen in the drawing room, whereupon my father gladly welcomed me and helped me to a chair. "You are feeling better?" he inquired, pouring my tea.

"I feel some improvement, thank you," I replied.

"As I told your father," Sir Edward put in, "English blood like yours quickly rallies. Perhaps we might have our expedition today, then?"

"Our expedition?" I looked from his pleased expression to my father, who had the grace to blush.

"Sir Edward has asked if we could walk with him to

the bay," he said. "So as to show us what he has in mind. I thought, perhaps, we could take the cabriolet, and he could ride—"

"Nonsense," Sir Edward interrupted. "It is hardly any distance, and the fresh air would be the perfect tonic for Miss Daniel's indisposition."

Unbidden, the clippings loomed in my mind once more. The murders had all happened on coastal paths, far from any help. And yet … the thought of striding freely through the countryside, as my father's companion rather than merely his daughter, was utterly compelling.

"I cannot think it wise for a young woman to go traipsing—" my father began.

"Look at her!" cried Sir Edward. "She is in fine fettle, perfectly capable. Aren't you, Miss Daniels?"

There was a note of challenge in his voice, a half-smile on his lips, and I found myself saying, "Of course I am," before I could properly think it through. But there was nothing for it. I could not bear to change my mind and give my father more cause to fret over me. All I could do was to ask for Mrs. Simmons to help me change my clothes, and instruct her carefully on where we were going, how long we might be, and when to send Mr. Simmons to ascertain our situation.

Not even the fear of death could undo the blustery drama of the day, or how good the spongy earth felt beneath my feet. It had rained in the night, leaving the world shimmering as if painted in dew. The air was invigorating, the scuttling clouds as awe-inspiring as a church. When Sir Edward pointed out my high color to my father, his voice ringing with approval, I even found myself smiling in return. He was a strange man indeed, a decidedly unnerving one, but a murderer? It seemed impossible that this melancholic gentleman could be in any way responsible for the ghastly crimes Miss Chase had sent to me. That I had given an iota of credence to her accusations seemed ridiculous now.

We kept up a good pace across the fields and the last few copses before the start of the coast. I had deliberately loosened my stays and breathed deeply with every stride, and it was marvelous. Thankfully, Diana was not there to witness my pinking skin and my poor figure. The thought of her scolding me made me stifle a laugh.

As we walked, my father and Sir Edward kept up a conversation about trade and the colonies, and it warmed my heart to see my father so animated. Only now did I understand how limited his society had become in the years following my mother's death. The villagers were good people, but their conversation was fixed upon the same subjects—the weather, their dealings with markets and merchants, and gossip. I knew my father had traveled before marrying, and when I was very young he would often go to town with Uncle Stuart. Losing my mother had circumscribed his world, and those borders had grown smaller over time. It was no wonder that he was so taken with Sir Edward's company, and hopeful of some stronger connection between them.

When at last we came in sight of the water, I sighed aloud

with delight. The regular crests of the waves, the endless blue sky right to the horizon—they undid all my dark imaginings at once, for what horror could lie beneath such beauty? I had not been to the coast since well before the winter, and I had not realized how much I missed it. The crisp air made my skin tingle and my heart race. It was life, life, and I knew that no matter what, I would insist upon these walks going forward.

As I stood there, savoring the moment, it struck me: the birds still hadn't returned. No gulls careened over the water, nor had a note of song touched the air for the entirety of our walk.

"Stunning, is it not?"

Sir Edward's voice jolted me out of my thoughts. He was suddenly close, very close, and I repressed an instinctive shudder. "You were correct, sir," I said. "The air has revived me wonderfully. Only I cannot think why the birds haven't returned."

"The birds?" He frowned at me.

"They flew inland some days ago, and we have not seen one since."

"Why, it is the wrong time of year for sea birds," Sir Edward replied promptly. "They migrate further north in the warmer months. Most coastal birds do."

I knew this to be wrong, but I could not think of how to say it without sounding argumentative. I looked for my father, but he had moved away from us, and was intently studying the horizon with a little smile on his face. Sir Edward took my arm and steered me in the other direction, close to the cliff's edge, and I tensed in anticipation.

"Your father," he said in a low voice, "is intent that you

come to your own decision."

I swallowed. "I cannot think what you mean."

"About the bay." He stopped and pointed, turning me like a doll until I was following his arm to his satisfaction. "I think we can shore the land here, and add stairs down. There is enough of a beach below to drive the first pilings in, and then we can work from the start of the pier to extend it out."

"Oh!" I felt a rush of relief. "Yes, I see. Only I cannot but think the cost would exceed any fishing profits we might recoup."

"You misunderstand me," he said. "My interest in your property, and this bay, is purely to further my own business." He had stepped even closer to me; I could feel the heat of his breath on my ear. "My brother and I have many trading partners. It would be to our advantage to have a dedicated pier for our merchandise, one that would spare us the delays of inspections."

I looked at him then, trying to keep my tone light. "Why, Sir Edward! Don't tell me you are a smuggler after all?"

"I assure you, Miss Daniels," he said, "my activities have the *highest* approbation."

"That will be a relief to your wife, should you marry," I replied.

He looked at me then, and it was the same dark stare as when he had been reading to me. I could see a faint line of sweat at the edge of his wig, despite the blustery day. "Any wife of mine, Miss Daniels," he said quietly, "would serve God and country, as I do."

I cannot say exactly what happened then. I felt not pushed

exactly, but nudged forward, as if a breeze had blown solely at my back. Sir Edward caught me as I slipped forward with a cry of alarm, sending a shooting pain through my hand. I glimpsed the frothing waters of the bay below me, and what looked for all the world like a vast, dark shape, curved in mimicry of the bay's edge, before I was violently jerked back onto safe ground.

My father rushed towards us as Sir Edward quickly led me away from the edge. When I opened my hand, a short, deep cut ran across the rise of flesh below my thumb, a line that was quickly obscured by my rising blood.

"Caroline!" my father cried. "Caroline, are you all right?"

"I just lost my balance," I said quickly. "I'm fine, really, only I cannot think how …"

Sir Edward pressed his handkerchief over my wound. "This is my doing, I'm afraid," he said with an appropriately contrite expression. "One of my buttons has a sharp edge. You must have grabbed it when I steadied you." He held out the cuff of his coat sleeve, where there was indeed a button with a broken edge. Yet, what I had felt was a distinctly stabbing pain.

He eased away the handkerchief, showing a bright red blot, and my father gasped. "We must get you back to the house."

"It's just a cut," I said, trying to sound as reassuring as possible. "I will be fine, I promise."

But he was already hurrying me back towards the trees while fumbling for his own handkerchief. As we left, I glanced back to see if Sir Edward was following. He was carefully knotting the bloody handkerchief around something the size of a man's fist—a stone? As I watched, he tied it; then, with a great stretch of his arm, flung the kerchief and its weight out into the water. Only then did he turn and fall into step behind us, soon catching up with long strides, whereupon he took turns with me in reassuring my father that my injury was most unremarkable.

As we walked, an idea came to me. I turned to Sir Edward and asked him for the handkerchief. "Mrs. Simmons has a knack for removing such stains," I said. "And if she cannot, I would be pleased to replace it."

"It is no matter, Miss Daniels," he replied, patting his pockets. "I think I dropped it in my haste. Certainly, it is not on my person. It is probably floating away on the tide as we speak."

It wasn't the truth, but it wasn't a complete lie either, and I could not think of what else to say.

CHAPTER VIII

A Second Dinner

That afternoon I sat down to dinner with my hand neatly bandaged and a full glass of wine for my suffering. After some solicitous comments about my injury, my father turned the conversation back to the previous topic—which was, unsurprisingly, the profit that might be gained from leasing our coastline to Sir Edward. My father's eagerness made me wince, but I, too, was intrigued to hear just what this man might offer us.

"My brother and I determined many years ago that our most financially sound path lay in the Atlantic trade," Sir Edward said. "It is the foundation of our Empire. It can bring an Englishman nothing but benefit, for to invest in this trade is to invest in the lifeblood of England. We turned our complete attention to the sea and how we might best nourish England's prospects, and thus our own."

"Of course, of course," my father said. His face was ruddy and I wondered how many glasses he had imbibed already. "We are nothing without the sea."

"Exactly." He beamed at my father. "That is exactly right, Theophilus."

His patronizing tone, the way he looked at my father—

"When you say the Atlantic trade," I said sharply, "you are talking about the trade in men, are you not? You are talking about slavery."

They both looked at me with surprise, as if they had forgotten I was there. "Men, cotton, rum, sugar … it is all part of the same lifeblood." Sir Edward gave me an appraising look. "I see you find the business distasteful. But I assure you, they are not men and women like ourselves. Those we can, we lift into civilization; those who cannot be lifted, must serve. It has always been thus throughout history."

Though I could not claim intimate knowledge of the issue, I had read enough, between the newspapers and the pamphlets circulating in town, to know that many learned men believed it as abominable as it looked to my uneducated eye. "I wonder, Sir Edward, that England needs to engage in such a trade at all," I said. "Surely our wealth and our might at sea are enough to ensure the comfort of one small island?"

"To check our ambition is to spell our doom, Miss Daniels," Sir Edward replied. "Remember that Rome fell only when she had inscribed her borders and said, no further. Once you put boundaries on a man? You may as well bury him." He had picked up his knife and was turning it over and over. "For the good of England, we must press ever outward, we must fight and seize, we must conquer—no matter the price. Believe me when I tell you that England has higher powers to appease than mere morality."

"Your rhetoric has been honed in coffee houses and clubs, Sir Edward," my father said. "It is stronger than what we are used to here."

"And you are reaping the harvest of such weakness," Sir Edward retorted. "The poverty and idleness that has befallen this county is what I fear for the whole of England, should we yield any facet of our superiority—"

"Sir," my father said. Despite his tipsiness, there was a firmness in his voice that I had not heard for some time. "My daughter is at the table."

His tone brought Sir Edward up short. He hesitated, then carefully laid down his knife. "Forgive me," he said. "It has been some time since I've been in gentler society. I am certain my manners will only improve with the excellent examples you both provide."

Another might have been mollified by his words—certainly my father appeared to be. For myself, however, I felt rigid with an amorphous fear, filled with dread for something I struggled to clarify in my own mind. The man who spoke now of hiring workers and business plans seemed different from the one who had just spoken so vehemently about conquest. I could not help but think that this refined, polite Sir Edward was a mask, hiding another within—and that the hidden Sir Edward, who could casually deal in men as if they were livestock, who had conjured that hideous vision at the dinner party, would have no compunction about slitting a woman's throat.

I locked my door again that night.

CHAPTER IX

Departures

When I awoke in the morning, it was to the wonderful sound of the carriage returning.

For the first time in days, I dressed with enthusiasm, then sat patiently while Mrs. Simmons changed the dressing on my hand. It was an ugly cut, far worse than anything a rough button edge could have done. How had it happened, and why had Sir Edward behaved so strangely? The questions pressed upon me, and yet the prospect of simply closing the door on the whole strange visit was far more appealing.

When I came downstairs, it was to find the house in a state of disorder. Mr. Simmons and the coachman hurried past me on the stairs—to pack Sir Edward's things, Mr. Simmons explained. My father was busily pulling books from the library shelves and calling out their names to an absent Sir Edward, who was in the dining room with Miss Chase, the lease papers strewn over the table. I demurely helped myself to toast, avoiding Miss Chase's stare, and withdrew to the drawing room to wait out the chaos.

I had not been in the room since Sir Edward arrived. Now, I found it in a terrible state of disarray, with the chairs pushed against the farthest wall—there were distinct scrapes in the parquet that made me wince—in order to bare the floor for the display of several large maps. Some I recognized at once, for they were simple county surveys; others showed the lines of our property as they had been redrawn after my father sold off the last of several parcels. One map in particular had been singled out and placed upon a table, framed by empty wine glasses and held in place by a large magnifying lens. At first glance, it seemed an odd intersection of lines sketched over an old map encompassing our house, the Fitzroys', the bay, and the coach road, with Harkworth Hall at the center. All the lines seemed to run to the Hall, like a spider surrounded by its web.

The tunnels.

The one common fact in all the stories about the Hall was that the ground beneath the house was riddled with cellar rooms and tunnels. The kitchen, I knew, was lined with doors, at least half a dozen leading to cellars that led in turn to tunnels and passageways. Some simply ran to outbuildings, sparing servants from crossing the gardens in bad weather. One used to run to a hillock near the coach road, but had collapsed.

And, as my father had described, one opened up directly onto the bay, though a break in the line seemed to indicate damage.

I traced one in particular, running from the southwest corner of the Hall into the gardens. It was the one I had become lost in during that last summer day at the Hall. I had become bored with the games and wandered into the kitchen, where I found a door slightly ajar. All these years later I could still remember the dusty cellar and the gaping tunnel mouth, how the air in the passageway had tasted foul and wet. Several steps into the darkness and I had lost all sense of direction, and ran forward in a panic. After what felt like a lifetime, I had emerged sobbing into a little stone circle engulfed in flowering vines. I believed myself dead and in Heaven ... but then the tunnel door slammed shut on me, and I could not find another way out of what turned out to be an overgrown folly. The servants found me by my crying, and I had been secretly relieved when the Archers quit the house.

Looking around our drawing room now, I understood that what I was seeing was an attempt to intimately understand the county, both its physicality and its residences. Perhaps my jab about smuggling was closer to the mark than I knew.

A cough made me start. I whirled about to see Miss Chase standing in the doorway. She bowed slightly, but her gaze was fixed on the bandage on my hand, so intently that I drew it close to my chest.

"Miss Daniels," she said. "Your father—he sent me to find you, we are about to depart." She was frowning as she spoke, and suddenly she blurted out, "You cut your hand?"

"It's merely a scratch," I retorted. "I am sorry you must depart so soon," I added, in a tone that made it clear I was anything but.

She seemed not to hear me. "How did it happen?"

"I cannot imagine—"

"How?" Her expression was grim.

"I—I nearly fell, while we were walking," I said. "Sir Edward caught me. He said one of his buttons was broken, the edge must have cut my hand." I bit my lip, then added in a rush, "It is far too deep, though, for such an explanation. And afterwards, the handkerchief—"

But I stopped when she raised her hand. She looked outside the room, then closed the door partway and drew close to me. "It had your blood on it?" she asked in a low voice.

"Yes," I admitted.

"Were you close to the water, and did he throw it in afterwards?"

"How did you know?"

"You would not believe me if I told you," she said, then added quickly, "and we cannot tarry here, he'll be suspicious of any delay. Only, I beg of you, do not pursue any further relationship with Edward Masterson. His interest is not what you think, and you put yourself at great risk should you align your interests to his."

She was already opening the door, shooing me out of the room. Once outside, though, I pointedly waited until she took my arm, forcing us to walk closely together to the main doors. I took very small steps that slowed her to nearly a shuffle.

"You sent me those clippings," I whispered, keeping my gaze straight ahead.

"I did." She too kept her gaze ahead, pretending to look at our walls.

"Do you honestly believe he killed those women?"

"He is a likely suspect."

"Then why do you work for him?"

"That, I cannot tell you." She smiled and nodded as my father appeared in the doorway.

"Does it have to do with why you dress like—like *that*?"

I felt her whole body go rigid and her arm left mine. "I dress as I please," she hissed. "If you think my breeches an offense on a par with murder, Miss Daniels, then you are not the woman I took you for."

"Then we are even," I whispered back, suddenly furious, "since you are not the man I took you for, nor the man my father still believes you to be. Such impropriety may be acceptable where you come from—"

But I could not finish my tirade. We were at the doors, and she abruptly halted and kissed my hand. "Miss Daniels," she said curtly, and strode past me into the light.

I followed her out onto the porch, only to be surprised. A second vehicle had crowded into our drive: the familiar landau of the Fitzroys. Diana was just being helped out by Uncle Stuart. She waved to me and I waved back. Beside me, Miss Chase took her leave of my father, shaking his hand, and then retreated to wait by the carriage. Sir Edward was greeting Uncle Stuart while Mr. Simmons helped the coachman lash the last of his luggage to the vehicle.

"I like that fellow," my father murmured in my ear, nodding at Miss Chase's back. "He's got a good head on his shoulders, that one."

I could not help but follow his gaze, watching Miss Chase as she settled her hat upon her head and twitched her lapels straighter. Her expression was uneasy as she watched how Uncle Stuart clapped Sir Edward on his shoulder, how Diana rushed up to hug me.

"Darling," she said in my ear, "for goodness' sake, stop

staring! What will Sir Edward think?"

At once, I averted my gaze, too flustered to think of a reply. Thankfully Diana caught sight of my bandage and set to kissing my hand with a little cry of dismay. The soft press of her lips, how she fussed—it was charming, and yet at the same time discomfiting, and I found myself glancing at the carriage once more.

Miss Chase met my gaze directly. She smiled, a strangely sad smile, but before I could react my gaze was cut off by Sir Edward's looming form. "As I was telling your father," he said without preamble, "it is my sincerest hope that you will let me repay your kind hospitality and be my first guests at Harkworth Hall. Say, in a week's time?"

"We would be delighted," my father replied, beaming. "Perhaps we can all come, eh, Fitzroy?"

"My father has to be gone for some days," Diana put in, "but I'm sure we can join you later."

"Following up on some of your recommendations, Sir Edward," Uncle Stuart added. "I can bring my news with me when we join you and perhaps we can come to some arrangements."

At the word *arrangements*, Diana stifled a giggle and my cheeks flared with heat. Everyone looked at Sir Edward, but I could not bring myself to do so. I dreaded seeing his re-action. Oh, I had thought us done with it all, at least for a time. How was it that I was suddenly to be at Harkworth Hall in a matter of days, with only my father by my side?

Now Sir Edward took my hand, with a careful, almost formal gesture, and raised it to his lips. Their touch, though brief, nearly made me shudder, and it was all I could do to keep the same empty smile on my face, keep my gaze on the vista just past his ear. "Then it is decided," he said. "You will be my first, my most special guest, Miss Daniels. I will be counting the days."

With a last bow, he turned and strode towards his carriage. Diana gave my arm a squeeze. "All bespoke, and that suit is French," she purred in my ear. "And you are to be his most special guest? I call that a successful visit, despite you wearing your stays so loose."

"Diana," Uncle Stuart said reprovingly, but a smile was playing around his lips.

"A great man," my father said, as the carriage rolled away. "A very great man indeed. A glass of something, Fitzroy, Diana?"

They assented, but as they turned to go inside I clutched at Diana's arm. "Are you certain about Sir Edward's character?" I asked. "Does nothing seem strange about him?"

"Caroline!" There was a hint of exasperation in her tone. "You have been alone in the country for far too long. He is a fine gentleman and you are exactly what he needs." At the last, she caught herself, softening her voice. "Not everyone can be a princess, darling," she said more gently. "He is doing great work on behalf of England. It is no small thing to help him in this."

She gave me a swift kiss, then followed the men inside. Still, I lingered on the porch, running my thumb over the cut on my hand, quietly furious. Neither princess nor pirate, indeed; merely a ninny. I had simply let them plan, I had not spoken up; too, I had wasted that valuable time with Miss

Chase. I could have asked her anything—how did she know about the handkerchief? What other criminal acts did she suspect Sir Edward of? Instead, I had attacked her over her clothing, professing outrage when, in truth, my real outrage was that my father could so easily accept her as an equal, while I could barely be suffered to walk a few miles on our own property. Now, I had only my suspicions, where I might have had facts to guide me.

When I finally went inside, I passed the library where my father had taken the Fitzroys and hurried instead to the kitchen to apprise Mrs. Simmons of the change in visitors. When I entered, it took me a moment to find her. She was huddled on a chair in a corner, weeping profusely, her face buried in her apron.

"Mrs. Simmons?" I hurried to her side and wrapped my arms around her. "Dearest! Whatever is the matter?"

"It's Emily, Miss," she managed, her voice shuddering. "Yesterday, she went up to Harkworth Hall, to put in her name for employment now that it's let. But they say she never arrived and no one's seen her since, and there's not hide nor hair of her anywhere by the road." She looked at me, her eyes reddened and full. "Everyone fears the worst."

CHAPTER X

A Reply

I could not sleep that night. My hand throbbed unmercifully, though it had barely stung the previous night. Again and again I dreamed of the sea, of the roaring waves and that great eye beneath the surface. Only now, instead of myself falling in, it was Emily, and I was reaching, reaching out to seize her as she disappeared into the churning surf—

And then I would awaken, sweating and with a pounding heart, only to repeat the exercise.

At last, I awoke sometime before dawn with my mind awhirl. It was possible that Emily had simply suffered an accident—perhaps she had cut across country, perhaps she had fallen. But she was a native of these parts … and that she had been bound for Harkworth Hall was too great a coincidence. But how could I explain my suspicions to anyone? I had nothing for proof save a few pieces of paper, Sir Edward's odd behavior, and the dark hinting of Miss Chase—whose motives were as suspect as his.

As I was leaving my room to go to breakfast, I found Mr. Simmons striding towards me and I hurried to meet him. "There is news?" I asked hopefully.

But he only shook his head. "A letter for you, Miss. It

came on the first post," he explained as he handed me the envelope. "I thought you would want it right away, since it was sent so urgently."

I did not recognize the hand, but the marks upon it told me it came from the next county. My letter, it seemed, had provoked a response, faster than I had imagined.

"I was hoping, Miss, if you didn't need Missus Simmons, she could come with me this afternoon," Mr. Simmons said. "To stay with her sister. What with Emily still missing …"

"Of course." At once I felt a fool for not suggesting the very thing. They could have been away at first light. "Of course you can both go. Take all the time you need."

His reddened eyes were filling; the sight made my own throat close. With a last, awkward nod I went back to my room clutching the envelope, but I did not open it until I heard Mr. Simmons' steps fade downstairs. Only then did I break the seal and read.

Dear Miss Daniels,

I hope this reply does not shock you with its rapidity—as you were writing out of concern for a houseguest, I wanted to reassure you at once. Your memory of my poor sister's circumstances is slightly mistaken. Her husband was a Mr. Theodore Masters, not Edward Masterson. The similarity is striking, and it is natural that your mind should have leapt to uneasy conclusions. Indeed, Mr. Masters would have been about the same age as your houseguest, and seems of a similar background, for he too had been a self-made merchant of substantial means. But

I believe were we to visit London, we would meet a dozen such men, similar in both name and person—and yet without the peculiar combination of traits that comprised Mr. Masters. Unlike most rational men, he had a particular interest in ancient tales, especially Biblical apocrypha. Indeed, he even called the shipping firm he founded, "Leviathan." I daresay your Edward Masterson would rightfully scoff at such eccentricities.

As for unusual circumstances regarding my poor sister's death: the only unusual aspect was that it happened at all. My sister was a timid creature, discomfited by large gatherings and most at ease in our conservatory with its harpsichord. Mr. Masters insisted on their taking daily walks along the coast, which he believed would strengthen her constitution. That she sought to please her husband by accompanying him is a testament to her wifely devotion, but I have never understood why she chose to walk out alone when he was on the Continent on business. It seems the actions of a completely different person—! God willing, one day we will meet again, and I can ask her why she went out that fateful night.

My sincerest hopes that this finds you in good health and puts to rest any concerns you might have. I am grateful that my sister's fate, however dreadful, still lingers these ten years later, as a caution to young women everywhere.

Yrs sincerely,
James G—

I read it over twice, with care, my dread growing with each review. Instead of putting to rest my concerns, the letter brought them into sharper relief. The names were far too similar to be coincidence. The death was distant enough that few would associate Edward Masterson with his previous self. The interest in lore seemed in keeping with a man who would make such speeches about England, or enjoy such lurid poetry. Again, I felt the blade against my throat, the sudden searing pain, and the terrible fall into the icy depths where that great eye watched.

Leviathan.

The eye … but here, my mind balked at the prospect: I could envision a man with such an untoward obsession, I could envision him crafting some complex motive for murder, but that there could be such a beast? More likely Sir Edward suffered from some kind of madness that possessed him of such fantastic ideas—and that he could twist his own gift of rhetoric to inflict those ideas on others.

Inflict his ideas, and far more. The letter had taken my inclination and made it certainty. Somehow I needed to ascertain the truth, for both Emily's sake and my own … even if it meant going to Harkworth Hall.

CHAPTER XI

Follies

That morning, I helped Mrs. Simmons pack a small satchel, then saw them both off in a neighbor's cart to go to her sister's house. As I had hoped, the neighbor had news, though none of it was good: the villagers had searched the countryside throughout the previous day and started again this morning, with still no sign of Emily. They had even searched the grounds and outbuildings of Harkworth Hall with Sir Edward's enthusiastic permission, with no results. The Hall itself had supposedly been locked until yesterday evening, and there were no signs of a forced entry. This explanation had satisfied everyone, it seemed, but it did not satisfy me.

I made my father and I a light breakfast while trying to think the whole business through. The gruesome images of Miss Chase's clippings, the stark description of the letter, all swirled in my mind, now with a helpless Emily in the role of victim, now myself, each of us tumbling into the cold waters of the bay. Still, I hesitated to act alone: surely there must be some way to suggest that the villagers search the Hall itself, or the nearby shoreline, without having to explain in detail—and possibly branding myself a madwoman.

I found my father poring over a set of notes Sir Edward had left behind, detailing his proposal for the bay. That he did not so much as glance at me when I put breakfast at his elbow told me he planned to be engrossed for some hours. Indeed, I had to clear my throat three times before he finally looked up.

"They're still searching for Emily," I began hesitantly.

"Ah, yes." He leaned back in his chair and rubbed at his temples. "Perhaps now you can understand why I am so loathe to let you wander on your own? This countryside has its dangers, especially for young women."

"I thought perhaps she might have gotten into the Hall," I said. "Through one of the tunnels. Or perhaps she's trapped inside one that collapsed."

My father only smiled at this dire image. "I know how much that day frightened you," he said gently. "But truly, Caroline, it is much closer to what your Uncle Stuart was describing. Any tunnel that was bound to collapse has already done so, and most were sealed off by different tenants over the years. The chances of her finding an open one are quite small. And if she had made her way into the Hall somehow, Sir Edward would have found her—I'm sure he searched the house thoroughly." He beckoned me close and took my hands in his. "It is very good of you to be so worried, but it seems to me the most likely explanation is that she was never bound for Harkworth Hall in the first place."

"Whatever do you mean?" I asked, startled.

"She's a young, pretty girl, Caroline. Serving girls especially are flighty things, they get their heads turned in the blink of an eye." When I still looked confused, he squeezed my hands. "I mean that it's most likely she ran off with a fellow, for better or worse."

"But her family relies on her wages," I said. "She has three little siblings! She wouldn't have abandoned them."

My father only gave me a knowing look, then squeezed my hands once more before releasing them. "Well. If she is to be found then they will find her, I'm certain of it."

His voice had a note of dismissal. I started to speak again, but what could I say? To press my case would be to cast aspersions on a valued friend, and, in truth, I did not want to see my father hurt a second time. He had been so withdrawn after my mother died, so distant. I did not want to lose his affection again.

He was engrossed in the notes once more, muttering to himself and scribbling in the margins. I could wait for news, I could wait for the Simmonses to return … but it might already be too late.

It was the work of a few minutes to change my dress into something plain and serviceable and my shoes for an old leather pair my mother had worn for walking. A hooded cloak completed my costume. I left a brief note claiming that I was walking to Diana's in the hopes of hearing more about Emily. Hopefully it would mitigate my father's concerns if he believed me merely at the Fitzroys'.

As for what I would do once I reached Harkworth Hall, I could not rightly say. How would I explain myself if confronted by Sir Edward, or Miss Chase? My resolve quavered at the thought, but I told myself that surely when the time came I would know how to act.

I set out with a satchel containing a little food, skirting the windows of the drawing room so as to avoid notice by my father. The walk, however, was more difficult than I remembered. We had only walked to the Hall a few times in my youth, and I had forgotten the uneven land, and how strong the winds could be. The gusting, briny air left me breathless; the rocky dirt hidden beneath the knee-high grasses threatened my knees and ankles. The satchel quickly became a dead weight on my shoulder, my skirts a veritable yoke I was dragging through the resistant vegetation. Too, I had not walked such a distance in far too long; it took far more endurance than the short bursts of housework I typically performed. Even the fierce beauty of the land could not distract me from how grueling the journey was, and I thought several times to turn back. But then Emily might be lost forever, and soon I would face my own dark fate at the Hall.

These grim musings carried me the rest of the way, but the sun was well past its peak when I finally came in view of the copse-dotted hollow and the slate rooftops of Harkworth Hall. And here was another unexpected aspect of the journey: how I was promptly assailed by memories of my mother, memories that only intensified as I drew closer to the house. My last visit here had been the party where I wandered into the tunnel, but my mother and I had made several visits that summer, exploring the gardens and visiting with the Archers. I had let my fright overshadow all other memories of the Hall, but to look before the day of the party was to find many happy recollections, each marked by my mother's easy laugh and welcoming arms. There had been so many other people in the county, then. I had never wanted for playmates. All gone now; our county was long since out of fashion. Families now looked for country homes farther south and west, closer to town and the better-kept coach roads.

Only then did I realize that I had avoided these memories not only to spare my father, but to spare myself.

I reached the last copse of trees before the gardens. From my vantage, I could see the lawn where we had played games, and the shady, rose-filled nook where the mothers would retire for tea and gossip. It was all sadly overgrown; how my mother would have wept to see it so unkempt! But try as I might, I could not spot the folly. My childish cries of panic had been heard, so therefore it should have been close to the house. Yet I could spot no round building, or any kind of structure that might include the door I remembered. Perhaps it had been filled in and razed.

As I crept through the gardens, I took advantage of the afternoon shadows to keep myself hidden. I was still teasing out memory from the moment, and thus did not notice the folly until I was nearly upon it.

Whatever the walls had been, they were now pulled down by the vigor of the vines I remembered, creating a spray of crumbled stone choked with vibrant green. But the floor remained, though cracked and crisscrossed with vines, and in its center was an angled door, set in a frame of mossy stone. The door of my childhood. Yet it seemed impossible that a small child such as myself should have pushed open such a heavy slab of wood, and at such an angle. Had the door been left open? I distinctly remember pushing it and having it open easily, like a door in a house. Or had there been another tunnel, another folly? For a moment, I felt overcome by doubts: of my memories and perceptions, of my purpose in coming here.

But, God help me, I could not turn back. For Emily's sake, if not my own.

As if in agreement, a sudden breeze rushed through the gardens, making the trees rustle pleasantly. It felt dreamlike to pick my way through the vines and step onto the stone circle, and though it was no longer the enclosure of my youth, still I shuddered to find myself standing there once more. I had to step over more vines to reach the door. Situating myself to best draw it open, I found myself thinking not of my living mother but of her coffin, as it had been lowered into the earth ...

Oh, even the rustling leaves seemed muffled. Truly my child-self had been right in one instance: it was another world within the folly, one that seemed smothered of all life.

Smothered of life. It struck me then: the chimneys. I studied the roof of the Hall, but there was not a hint of smoke, nor did I recall seeing any on my approach, not even from the outbuildings. Yet who, upon taking possession of a property, would leave the fires unlit?

Resolved to be more observant, I pulled on the door, but the handle was slippery with dew, the surrounding stone slick with moss. When I threw the fullness of my strength into the movement my feet slid from beneath me. I fell one way, the satchel flew in another, and I found myself sprawled on the stone with my food strewn about. Once I struggled to my feet again I was smeared with dirt and moss, a fine addition to my muddy hems and shoes, and my food inedible.

I felt foolish ... and then I was angry. I had not come all this way to be defeated by a door. Bracing my feet properly this time, I strained at the heavy wood slab until at last it swung free, far more smoothly than I had expected. I gave a little cry of triumph. It fell to the side, baring its dark opening in a way that felt obscene. The hinges gleamed with oil, and there were oval marks on the steps leading down.

Someone had used the passage, and recently.

I took a deep breath. In all likelihood, it had been done by an agent, or Sir Edward himself when he was surveying the property. That my armpits were damp with sweat as I descended, that my heart fluttered in my chest, was all merely my own foolishness.

The passageway was as dark and humid as I remembered. Swaths of web clung to the edges of the ceiling and the broken paving glistened with moisture. Positioning myself with care once more, I swung the door up and closed behind me, using a stone to prop it open so I would have some light and air. I began to walk forward, my skirts catching on the damp walls. In all likelihood, I would find the house empty; in all likelihood, Sir Edward was a scoundrel, a rake, and nothing more.

For God's sake do not go anywhere alone with him.

The passageway dipped. The light from the door grew thin, then disappeared altogether. Now, I had to feel my way, letting my fingers slide along the moist walls. I stepped carefully, feeling for gaps in the paving stones lest I fall and injure myself. That would make a fine coda to my brief, unremarkable life: my corpse found in an illicit tunnel, midway to spying on a suitor. The thought set me giggling, and just then my foot skidded on something soft and wet. I felt a stabbing pain in my ankle as I nearly fell on my face, exactly as I had imagined. Cold wetness soaked into my skirts and my sleeve where I had grabbed at the passage wall. Taking a deep breath to calm myself, I wiped my wet hands on my skirts and continued on.

At last, I saw thin lines of light ahead, at first so faint as to seem a trick of my straining eyes, but as I drew close they elongated and swelled until finally they formed the approximate outline of a door. It was the work of a few minutes' careful exploration to seize upon an iron pull. There was not a sound from the other side save the soft whistling of air. I slowly eased the door open.

I found myself in a dusty cellar, dimly lit by small windows set near the ceiling. A spiral staircase led up into gloom. The room was empty save for some broken crates piled against a wall. As I crossed to the stairs, I glanced at the broken wood, then pulled a board free. Burned into it was a shape like a sun, with thick, sinuous rays, and beside it in large block letters, LEVIATHAN.

Indeed, he even called the shipping firm he founded, "Leviathan."

And there it was, in my hand: a physical link between Theodore Masters, murderer, and Sir Edward Masterson. I dropped the wood as if it was burning me, so sickened did I feel, only to see that my knuckles were spattered with what looked like flakes of rust. Leaning forward, I pushed away more of the broken wood, and found underneath a pile of dirty clothing and other rubbish—but it was the clothes that caught my eye. With some effort, I pulled free a large shirt, holding it up to the light—

—only to recoil at both sight and smell. I knew that vast stain, I knew the smell coming off it. The smell seemed to fill the air, as it had filled our house the night my mother died.

Blood.

I ran blindly up the stairs, my mind whirling. I had to get it off me. My mother's sightless eyes, the stained sheets beneath her spread legs. The monster in the red, red water. I had to get it off me.

At the top of the stairs, I burst into the far end of the kitchens. My gaze fixed upon the cistern—to get it off me, to get it all off me!—but it was empty. I looked around frantically for some other means to wash, but the afternoon sunlight testified to a room untouched for years: hearth and furniture thick with dust, beams swathed in delicate cobwebs, flagstones peppered with rodent droppings. Every hook and shelf was empty.

I took a deep breath, and another. Sir Edward had never intended to live here. He had never intended to live here at all.

Slowly, I wiped my hands as best I could on my skirts, willing myself to stay calm. That the blood was Emily's, that it spoke of villainy—but I had to be certain. They could as easily have killed an animal. Even the wooden crates, I saw now, could be dismissed as coincidence, or burned while I was getting help.

As I reasoned this through, my eyes kept roving over the kitchen. It was as I remembered, every wall punctured by doors, many of which were blocked by furniture. A few, however, were decidedly in use, with polished knobs and dirt on the floors before them. Now I saw with renewed unease that among the droppings were spots of brown; now I saw the smear along one of the table edges, punctuated by what looked like the marks of bloody fingers. Closer inspection revealed more stains on the floor and then a larger discoloration in a corner, in front of a padlocked door.

My heart was racing as I drew close. In the soft light, I saw a shape in the center of the stain, coiled like a small, dead animal. Only when I stood over it did I see that it was a clump of reddish-brown hair, clotted with dried blood and flecks of something else, something pale and leathery.

"Emily," I whispered.

The stain ran under the door. I felt faint, completely nerveless, as I pulled on the padlock, trying to wrench it open. There was not a key in sight.

"Emily," I said, as loudly as I dared.

I strained to hear through the wood, any hint of movement, of breath, of some indication that she lived. But there was only silence.

Somewhere in the Hall there had to be a key.

It was with this grim mandate that I searched the kitchen once more, then ascended the few stairs that led into the house, inching my way deeper into Harkworth Hall.

CHAPTER XII

Harkworth Hall

Though the main floor was as vacant as the kitchen, Harkworth Hall was decidedly occupied.

Room after room greeted me with the same vista: furniture swathed in canvas and windows shuttered and latched. Outside the kitchen, there were no more bloodstains, though the floors were marked with other debris: mud and leaves, but also gnawed bones, heels of bread, and empty wine bottles. Inside the main entrance doors, I saw several different sizes of footprints, which gave me pause. I had not anticipated so many. Was there a veritable gang to contend with? What, then, were the roles of Sir Edward and Miss Chase?

That she, too, might be complicit in Emily's suffering—for some reason, the thought was more upsetting than Sir Edward's criminality. Yet, something kept her by her employer's side. I could not but assume that she was as much to be feared as he was.

I looked in cabinets and closets, I checked mantelpieces and every tray and dish I saw, but there were no keys to be had. In all likelihood, Sir Edward kept them in his rooms, or perhaps he never let go of them at all.

In the conservatory, I found the most blatant display of

the men's presence and learned what manner of companions Sir Edward fraternized with. The room I remembered as my favorite in the house, a light, airy space decorated by a feminine hand, peaceful and inviting. Now it was a ruin of its former self. The large windows were pocked with holes, through which the wind stirred the various items scattered about like the spoor of animals: a table hastily uncovered for a card game and splattered with wax, old papers and cheap tobacco pipes discarded on every surface, and everywhere the bottles, wine bottles and spirit bottles and ale-jugs, even the remains of a cask sitting in the corner and framed by crimson splashes. I did not dare to examine the corners of the room. The smells alone told me what baser functions had been performed there.

The room did yield one useful item, though: a stout poker, well-made and of an impressive weight. If they wanted another victim, I would make them work for their prize.

With the poker at the ready, I made my way to the main hall and the stairs leading to the upper story. As I ascended, I thought not of what lay ahead, but of poor Emily. What had she done to warrant such attentions? Surely it would have been no matter to let her believe the house as yet uninhabited, and make the long walk back home. Had she seen something, discovered something, that threatened Sir Edward's designs? Why else would he risk harming her, with himself nearby and thus a suspect?

At the top of the stairs, I paused again, listening. Here, too, the rooms were deathly quiet. Was I alone, or were there villains behind every door? Were they stupefied by drink, or were they listening to me, as I was listening for them?

Behind the first door there were no villains, but, again, there was ample evidence of their numbers. Beside the disheveled bed were two other pallets, plus an astonishing amount of wadded-up linen, an overflowing chamberpot, and of course the ever-present drink bottles. As I moved from room to room, peeking into each one, I found myself disgusted not only by the repeated tableaux of debauchery, but by the violence being wrought on the house itself. To see it treated like a sty felt a personal insult. I groaned inwardly at the bath, whose floors were swelling from repeated overflow; I flinched at the sumptuous damask drapes used to smother a fire. Women, it seemed, were not the only victims of Sir Edward's schemes.

I passed the stairs to complete my search only to halt suddenly, as alert as a startled deer. For there had been a faint creak, discrete and pointed—precisely the sound of a body stepping on a loose floorboard.

Silently, I pressed myself into the shadows against the wall. The creak came again: definitely from a room at the far end of the hall. I swung the poker a few times, testing the weight and heft of it, and began inching my way towards the sound.

Beneath the edge of the farthest door, a shadow flickered, and I instinctively raised the poker as I advanced. As I took step after step, I imagined some fearful brigand on the other side—but was he readying himself as well, straining to hear my advance, or was he merely stumbling about, drunk?

Oh, poor Emily! Oh, my poor father and his hopes! All

was about to be decided, in no doubt the most terrible terms.

At the door, I took a last deep breath, then flung it open—

—and rushed into a dim, seemingly empty room. For a moment I stood bewildered, trying to make out the details of the orderly bedroom I stood in.

Strong arms seized me from behind, wrapping around me and swinging me wildly towards the bed. I swung the poker back and low and struck a leg, causing my assailant to cry out and release me. I tumbled headlong onto the bed and rolled in a tangle of skirts and poker all over the side, striking my head hard on the unyielding parquet. The world spun, lights flashed before my eyes, and all went briefly dark. When I opened my eyes again, it was to the glow of a lit candle. Quickly I righted myself, holding the poker out before me.

Only to find myself gaping at a disheveled Miss Chase, clutching her shin with one hand and a candlestick with the other, looking equally astonished.

"You!" she cried. "What are you doing here?"

"Where is Sir Edward?" I demanded at the same time. "What in God's name is happening in this house?"

Miss Chase seemed not to hear me; she kept gaping at me in bewilderment. "Why did you come here?" she asked, her voice nearly a wail. "I told you what kind of man he was, I told you what would happen!"

"You sent me three clippings with no particulars and did not even sign your name," I retorted. I could feel my face growing hot. "Did you honestly think I would believe *you?*"

As soon as I spoke I regretted my words. Miss Chase recoiled as if I had struck her, and then her expression darkened. "Of course, I forgot. You judge character by clothing." She took a deep breath. "And it does not matter. We must get you safely away."

"I am not leaving until you tell me what's become of Emily." I swung the poker in a wide arc, nearly striking the bedpost. "And what is the meaning of all of this."

"What do you mean, 'what's become of Emily?'"

"For God's sake, enough pretense!" I cried. "I know she is locked below. Tell me what he's done to her!"

For a moment, Miss Chase stared at me, her mouth open, and then she looked around the bedroom. "We have to find his keys," she gasped. "Or perhaps I can work the lock …"

She went at once to the desk in the corner, its surface strewn with papers, and without preamble began throwing them aside and opening the drawers. "How long has she been missing for?" she asked without looking at me.

I realized I was just standing there with the poker held out before me. "Two days now. We only got word last night."

"Damn! I think he has the bloody things with him." She stood up, frowning. "Let's check his coats, just to be sure. Though, two days …" she shook her head and my heart sank.

"But why her?" I tucked the poker under my arm and seized the nearest coat, hanging neatly on a chair, rifling through the pockets. Miss Chase had gone to the wardrobe and was feeling each garment in turn. "She hasn't a penny to her name."

Miss Chase paused, looking at me. "Why would that matter? He's not interested in money." She waved a hand at the bedroom. "He has more than enough sources of income."

I stopped in my search. "But then why does he kill them?"

"Isn't it obvious?" She shook her head. "He wants *them,* Miss Daniels. He wants their *blood,* he wants their *bodies.* Theirs and yours. Which is why you should leave here at once. I'll find Emily, though I doubt there's much left to find—good God, are you hurt?"

Her gaze had at last alighted on my filthy skirts and I found myself blushing. "I am perfectly all right," I snapped. "What do you mean, he wants their blood?"

"Did you *walk* here?" Her eyes went wide, as if some enormous discovery had just struck her.

"I hardly think the manner of my transit is the most pressing concern," I said, exasperated now.

"It may turn out to be, if you become his next victim solely for lack of a horse," she snapped.

"Tell me why he wants their blood!"

She looked darkly at the wardrobe, then kicked the door in visible frustration. "You would not believe me—"

"*Tell me,*" I cut in.

Glowering, she took a breath. "He believes there is a, a *creature*, that inhabits the waters between us and Europe. It protects us from invasion and in turn he feeds it … people. Preferably women, preferably Englishwomen." She ran a hand through her hair, loosening the queue. "And yes, I know, it's absurd. But he believes it and he is not the only one. His brother certainly believes it. And there are others."

"You must be joking," I blurted out. Though even as I spoke, I remembered the eye, and that vast form beneath the waves.

"I said you would not believe me."

I pressed on, ignoring the bitterness in her voice. "Who are these others, then? Bear in mind I have seen evidence of the kind of company you keep."

She smiled tightly. "His servants will do anything for drink and gambling money. I am speaking of other gentlemen, perhaps even a minister. Someone is funding Edward Masterson, perhaps many someones. There are large deposits at regular intervals, there are new identities, introductions, everything he needs to present himself anew in different social circles …" she trailed off.

"Theodore Masters," I said.

She was silent for a moment. "You, what? Wrote to the family?"

I nodded.

"And still, you came?"

"I could not let Emily suffer such a fate."

Again she fell silent, gazing at me, then shook herself. "Well. I think it's time for you to depart, and I am going to try to break that door—" but she silenced abruptly, her whole body trembling and alert as a pointer. "They're coming," she whispered.

"Who is coming?" I asked in alarm.

"Masterson and the others. We must hide you. Quickly," she added as I stood there, suddenly nerveless with fear. For I, too, heard it: just the faintest rumble of a vehicle on the road.

"Surely I can just …" I looked around, trying to find a hiding place in the sparsely decorated room. The wardrobe was stuffed to capacity, and there seemed to be no other egress.

"Not here," Miss Chase said. She seized my arm and dragged me to the door, pausing as she cautiously peered into the hallway. Now the sound was more pronounced: the thunder of many horses flying down the road, mingled with a carriage's rattle and decidedly male voices shouting and singing.

Suddenly, she pulled me across the hall and around a corner to where a small door was tucked into an alcove. Miss Chase opened it to reveal a narrow, dark staircase—a servant's stairs. As she made to lead me up, however, I balked. Who was to say she wasn't part of this conspiracy?

As if she could hear my thoughts, she turned around and held out her hand. "I am not party to his madness, Miss Daniels," she said in a low voice. "I cannot prove this to you. I can only give you my word. But consider that to try and sneak past his dozen followers is tantamount to suicide, while in the attic you would only have myself to contend with."

Still I hesitated, but the noise was upon us. Before I could think further, I hurried up the gloomy stairs, pushing past Miss Chase's outstretched hand. Behind me, I heard the door shut and bolt. When I reached the next floor, I stopped, letting her slide past me once more—and even though I was trembling with fear and anticipation, the momentary pressure of her body against mine seemed to agitate me in a new manner.

Behind me, Miss Chase lit two lamps. The room slowly revealed itself to be a large section of the attic, running in all directions into an echoing darkness. One lamp, she set upon a crude desk, the other, on the floor beside a narrow pallet. A change of clothes hung over a chair. There was little more, save furniture covered in canvas, several old chests, and a small, newer-looking trunk that I took to contain Miss Chase's personal effects.

"I know it's not much," Miss Chase said. "But you should be safe here. They never come up, save if they are in their cups and mistake my door for another."

A shout came from somewhere outside. Swiftly, she went to one of the low dormer windows ringing the space, careful to keep from standing directly before it. I came up behind her and peeked over her shoulder. The window afforded a partial view of the main drive before the house. I could see half a dozen men stumbling about, trying to maneuver horses and torches without relinquishing the bottles they clutched. Two were shoving each other; one finally tried to throw a punch, only to fall to his knees.

"Who are they?" I whispered.

"Brigands, for the most part," she replied in an equally low voice. "A few are well-born sons fallen from grace. They play the public roles. Two such would have greeted you upon your arrival as footmen, another as a butler." She laughed, soft. "And myself as secretary, of course."

"Is that how you serve him, then?" I asked in a low voice. "As a fallen son?"

She looked at me, then angled her head. "We need to get you out of those clothes."

"Pardon?" I felt my whole body flare with heat, as if every inch of my skin was blushing.

"You're the only person in this house in a dress, Miss

Daniels." She pushed past me and opened her little chest, rifling through the clothes and flinging piece after piece at me. "They're so drunk they probably won't realize you're not one of them—*if* you look the part. But those skirts will be a flag before a bull." She glanced up at me, her expression bemused. "I promise I won't look."

As much as I hated to admit it, her suggestion made perfect sense. With as much dignity as I could muster, I tucked my poker securely under my arm, then gathered up the breeches and waistcoat from the floor. "I will keep my own shift and stockings, thank you," I said firmly.

"Suit yourself." She went and dropped down on the pallet, her back to me. I looked around, then scurried behind what seemed to be a large wardrobe covered in canvas and began unpinning my dress.

"My father was Matthew Chase. You would know him if you resided in London. He was a prominent attorney." Her voice was low, but it carried. "He excelled at law, but he was terrible at managing his finances. When he passed away, I went to his creditors, presenting myself as his long-lost son, and was able to negotiate us out of debt. I even managed to parlay his firm into profit again—until Edward Masterson set his sights on my sister."

I shucked out of my dress and petticoat, then carefully stuck one leg into the breeches, followed by the other, trying not to squeal at the strange sensation of wool between my legs. "Go on," I said.

"At first we thought him merely a libertine. Once his seduction was complete, he demanded the usual vast monies to marry her—and to keep my sex a secret, for my foolish sister had told him everything." She took a deep breath. "My mother was terrified of the scandal and dispatched me to make arrangements. On my way to our rendezvous, I was seized by agents of the Crown, who placed before me the whole of his history, and the far darker fate that awaited my sister. They were eager to discover whose money was financing his schemes, and asked me to help them, in exchange for sending my sister and mother abroad. Spying seemed a small price to pay to ensure their safety."

"And it was so easy, to secure his employment?" I was buttoning up the waistcoat, but never had I felt so exposed. I lingered in the shadows, taking a few experimental steps—and in truth, I was also holding my breath, waiting for her response.

"He knew I had managed to clear my father's slate, and he believed I alone had managed my sister's flight," she said. There was a hint of anger in her voice. "I did not have to buy my post with my charms, if that's what you mean. I had already proven myself a dab hand at juggling numbers and bending laws. And, of course, it is a known fact that a woman like me lacks all scruples," she added dryly.

Now I, too, was irritated, both at myself and her. "A dab hand at bending the law, and committing violence as well?" I asked, ignoring her last remark.

She did not reply. I was still wriggling in my new clothes, trying to keep the waistcoat from twisting uncomfortably, when suddenly she was before me. She roughly pushed my hands down and took a step back. "That will do," she said. "Leave the bottom button undone if it starts riding up around your waist." She looked me over again, then suddenly grinned. "You left your stays on?"

"I certainly did," I replied hotly.

"Then you're a better woman than I. I cannot stand the damn things." She went to her chest and began rummaging again.

I frowned at that. "But you wore them at our house." At her confused look, I tugged on my own, mimicking her gesture from that day, and her confusion became a delighted grin.

"Is *that* what gave me away?" She gave a bark of laughter. "I was wondering. I happen to be wearing jumps, seeing as you're curious. Which, on the day in question, were full of fleas, thanks to that inn." She stood up, a pistol in one hand and a bag of shot in the other. "Come on."

"Where are we going?" I asked, still loathe to leave the shadows.

"To find Emily, of course—"

But she was interrupted by a braying voice echoed up the narrow stairs. "Chase! Chase, come here at once! Damn it all, where are you?"

"Of all the cursed luck," she whispered. Quickly she pressed both pistol and shot into my hands. "Load this," she ordered. "And do not leave until I return. I will be back as quick as I can—and perhaps I can get the keys as well. Do not leave until I return," she repeated, giving me a little shake. "You will be seized within moments without me to guide you, and these are not men to be trifled with."

I swallowed hard. The pistol in my hand was surprisingly heavy. "I understand," I managed.

She looked at me keenly, but Sir Edward's voice came again—for it was him, bellowing and cursing. His real voice, I realized, not the polished, dreamlike intonation he had used in my company.

Miss Chase started to speak, but stopped and instead bowed deeply before me. And with a last searching look she was gone, hurrying down the stairs, the key scraping in the lock and the door shutting once more.

CHAPTER XIII

The Door Unlocked

There was a time, I think, when the Caroline Daniels I had been would have done as she was told, even by a strange woman wearing breeches, even though she was wearing breeches herself.

But then again, that Caroline had also insisted on being taught to shoot, to load a gun and clean it, to handle both Mr. Simmons' ancient army pistol and my father's two hunting rifles. I busied myself now with loading Miss Chase's gun, a weighty thing with a long muzzle that was painfully clean and polished. Had she sat in this dim, lonely space night after night, cleaning her weapon and plotting her next steps? Or had she kept her pistol ready to defend her employer—defend, and perhaps even kill for him?

Oh, but her story had rung true to me. Yet, did I dare trust my instincts? What did I know of true deceit, of murderers and thieves?

Still, if I could not trust in myself, I should never have come at all.

The pistol loaded to my satisfaction, I quickly knotted my hair, then seized an old coat Miss Chase had left on the chair. A further search turned up her tricorn, which I fitted to my own head. Thus fully disguised, I started for the door—only to pause as I passed her open trunk. I could say that I was searching for more weapons with which to protect myself, but in truth, I desperately wanted some kind of proof of her story.

It took but a few minutes to search her effects, for she had nearly none: a few pieces of clothing, a small volume of history, and a handful of notes in a pocketbook completed her possessions. There were no letters or trinkets, hardly even a tailor's mark in the garments. I could see the sense in ridding yourself of everything personal before entering the service of a madman. But with the intent to undo him, or aid him?

It was only as I went to return her items that I looked again at the paper lining the bottom of the trunk. They were pages of foolscap, marked by the same neat cursive that had adorned my envelope that fateful morning. A lifetime ago, now. I lifted the first page out, squinting in the dim candle-light. Names and lines; it took me a moment to recognize a tree of ancestry.

A tree that ended with myself.

Quickly I brought the candle close. My parents' names, my grandparents, my great-grandparents ... it was accurate, as far as I could tell. I drew out the rest of the papers: each was an ancestral tree, ending in a woman's name. One, I saw, was the lady whose family I had written to, the ill-fated bride of Theodore Masters.

He wants their blood, *he wants their* bodies.

I could not see that we had any relations in common, though. Was it simply some kind of proof of Englishness? Certainly, the names seemed English enough, no hints of foreign tongues on any of the branches ...

Unnerved, I quickly returned them to their original places. With luck, it would be some time before she noticed any disruption.

And then, taking a deep breath, I headed for the stairs, the pistol tucked in my breeches and the poker in my hand.

As I descended, a sudden rush of noise filled the stairwell. A chorus of male voices was singing lustily, a howling singalong of a kind I had never heard before. My skin rose into gooseflesh. When I laid my hand upon the doorknob, they abruptly dissolved into raucous laughter. I stood there, my hand on the knob, trembling. So many, so close! And I, a mere slip of a woman in a worn suit, with a poker and a single shot. It was so far from the life I had known until now, so full of risk and danger ... my heart was pounding with fear, but also with a kind of wild excitement I had not felt since childhood. For the first time, I understood that this was the same excitement that drove men to race horses and fight pointless battles, to go to sea or into the army—or even turn to piracy. Looking down at myself, I realized I was the spit of that long ago etching of Mary Read, and the realization brought with it a wave of emotion. I felt as if I might fly apart; I felt *alive* in a way I had never felt before.

I opened the door. Slowly, silently, just a crack at first, just enough to peek out into the hall. There were lights under several of the bedroom doors, but the hall itself was empty. The trick, I told myself, would be to behave as if I belonged there. As if I was, in fact, Miss Chase.

With that in mind I took a deep breath and then stepped

into the hallway. I took the time to shut the door, the poker dangling from my hand, then turned and walked briskly down the hall, swinging the poker like a walking stick. The stairs before me were like a beacon in the darkness. If I could just make it …

A door opened behind me. I heard a step on the floor, then a gruff, "It's just Chase."

My heart was racing. I thought I might be sick. Would she usually turn and acknowledge them? Say something back? I turned my head slightly and nodded. I was at the stairs, I was nearly descending—

—and the door closed gently behind me.

I let out a long, low exhalation as I descended, only to pause near the bottom. For the ground floor was all noise and light, seemingly from everywhere: singing and shouting, the sound of furniture scraping and glass clinking and a kind of slapping and raucous laughter. The hall leading back to the kitchen suddenly seemed a terrifying gauntlet. Instead I peeked carefully over the banister, then darted to the open front door. I could go around the Hall and reach the kitchen from the side.

I will confess that the moment I stepped outside all my euphoria vanished, and I nearly turned and ran. The house with its blazing windows seemed a monster I could rightfully flee now; the thought of crossing the fields at night seemed a small concern compared to returning to the Hall. I could reach home before dawn and return with constables, neighbors, *help*—

—in which time Sir Edward and his men might have vanished, or at least removed all traces of their crimes. And what of poor Emily?

I slipped off the porch and began making my way to the side of the house, where I knew a door to the kitchen lay, only to see ahead of me on the path two large men coming straight at me.

I could not think, and then, by some unconscious instinct, I clutched at my groin and ducked into the bushes.

"Oi," one said. "What're you doing in there?"

I kept my back turned to the path. Their steps on the gravel were like some dread army approaching. Carefully, I moved the poker before me and gripped it tight with both hands, readying myself to swing.

"Not all of us can go with you watching, Tom," the other one said, then laughed loudly at his own joke.

"Is that Chase in there?" The footsteps had slowed. "Need a hand, girl? I'm happy to help."

I took a breath. "Bugger off," I snapped, in what I hoped was a decent imitation of her voice.

The second one laughed harder; I heard a hand slap a shoulder. "Go on, you creepy bastard," he said lightly. "You know she's not to be touched. Evening, Chase."

Again, I nodded. *She's not to be touched.* Images of her embracing Sir Edward, helping him, filled my mind, making my stomach churn. Yet, was that not preferable to her talk of monsters and blood? Unless the meaning was something even more sinister …

She's not to be touched.

What did Miss Chase's family tree look like?

I peeked out of the bushes. The path was empty. Quickly, I darted down and made for the kitchen door. It was farther than I remembered, around the corner and near the far end. Somewhere in the distance, I heard another man moving through the overgrown vegetation, but thankfully, he did not come near. A guard? I had not thought Sir Edward might post such. Perhaps my dash across the hills would have been short-lived.

At the door I touched my pistol, making sure its handle was at the ready, then gripped my poker firmly. The gun, I knew, was a last resort, for the noise would bring the whole of the Hall down upon me.

I put my hand on the old round knob and tried to ease the door open, but the wood had swollen. Taking a deep breath, I put my shoulder to the wood and gave it a hard push, only to nearly fall inside as it swung open with a pop. I caught myself and quickly brought the poker forward, ready to keep any attacking man at bay.

The kitchen was thankfully empty, though not in the same state as I had found it earlier. One of the overhead lamps had been lit, its several candles burning brightly, casting a yellow glow over the large space. Now, there were sacks of food-stuffs dumped on the tables, making smears in the dust; now someone had flung a bucket of water over the large stain, thinning the rust into brown and grey smears and pushing the hair into a corner like a small dead animal.

I shut the outside door and tiptoed towards the stain. The door was still locked. Carefully, I set the poker between the hasp and the lock itself and rocked the point back and forth, back and forth, trying to break it open. The sounds were excruciatingly loud in the silent kitchen. I could only pray that the revelry elsewhere would muffle my efforts.

So intent did I become on breaking the lock that I did not notice any approach until suddenly the inner door swung open, letting in a rush of sound from the Hall. A drunken man stumbled into the room, catching at one of the tables to steady himself as the door slowly swung closed behind him. I pressed myself as far into the shadows as I could manage, but there was nowhere to hide.

With a snigger he shook his head, then began pawing through the food, shoving a roll in his mouth as he tried to break apart a wedge of cheese.

Well-born sons fallen from grace. I could see it in this one: his threadbare coat had once been richly embroidered, some gold still glinting amidst the grime; his wig had been fashionable once; the sword that hung from his hip had lost every ornament, studded only with tarnish. His face should have been a handsome middle age, but his features were sunken and reddened by drink.

And then he looked directly at me, and in a heartbeat went from pitiful to terrifying.

"Who're you?" He squinted at me, a leer spreading over his features that distorted them horribly. "Who let you in?"

I tightened my grip on the poker. My mind would not work. It was like trying to turn a key in the wrong lock.

"A naughty little lad," he breathed. Slowly he came around the table, a hand on his sword. "A naughty little lad trying to get behind the door and see. O, what is Masterson up to?"

His voice took on a high-pitched, mocking tone. "O, what is Masterson doing with those girls?"

I was about to say—something, but at his words I shut my mouth and instead willed him to keep talking.

"Oh, it cannot be true, can it?" He grinned then, baring yellow, broken teeth. "Deals with the devil, a hellbeast, sacrifices—cor blimey, guv'nor, it just can't be true." The last made him snort with laughter. "'Tis a pity it only likes the ladies, boy, or I would show you just what truth looks like."

He lunged for me. I swatted him aside with the poker and ran blindly across the kitchen, not knowing which way to go, thinking only to keep him at bay. He twisted faster than I expected, skidding and righting himself as he turned. A hand grazed my leg, then seized my ankle, bringing me down face-first onto the stone floor. The poker flew from my hand.

A fist landed on my lower back, so hard I could not breathe for the sudden pain. I cried out shamefully and kicked backwards. My foot connected with something and I heard a grunt as he fell against the table. Quickly, I dragged myself away, but he was upon me in an instant, grabbing at my arms and twisting me about as he tried to press me to the ground. All was chaos then, his hands wrenching me and I clawing and shoving at him while trying to get a purchase on the pistol—

—and then Miss Chase loomed behind him, and in one great arc swung the poker into his head.

He fell across me a dead weight. Warm wetness splattered on my face and upraised hands. I turned them over and saw the redness, I saw his cracked pate and the glistening flesh beneath. I heaved, my guts twisting so violently I thought I might faint. With an animal grunt, my assailant crawled away, fumbling for something under his coat. She raised the poker again and swung it a second time. There was a terrible sound, of something cracking wetly, and this time he fell and did not move.

I could not stop looking, looking at the blood everywhere, blood and brains. I could not breathe for it, I could see nothing else. Hands caught at me though I tried to push them away. Someone roughly turned me and I saw her, I saw Miss Chase and saw her mouth move, but I couldn't make out her words for the roaring in my ears. Her stricken face was before me, her eyes wide with concern, and then I was vomiting, vomiting, until there was nothing in my belly but sourness.

My hands kept wiping against my breeches, as if of their own accord.

"Are you all right?" Miss Chase's voice echoed, as if she was calling across a great distance. "Miss Daniels. Did he hurt you? Are you all right?"

"You—you killed—" I could barely speak for the way my whole body kept contracting. "You killed him," I finally said.

At once, her touch left me. She stood abruptly, her legs blocking my view of the body. I took deep breaths, steadying my nerves, steadying the world around me.

"He would have killed us both." Without further explanation, she bent over and seized him by the feet. I thought I saw her eyes gleaming, but she turned away and with a grunt, dragged him into a far corner. With some effort, she propped him into a sitting position, then took the hat that had fallen from my own head and placed it over his face. "That should buy us a little time," she said, striding past me and heading to the locked door.

"You killed him," I repeated.

She stopped then and looked at me. "He was wanted in London for murder," she said, "and if you had read what he did to that whore, you would have done exactly the same." She took a step towards me, her hand outstretched, and I instinctively recoiled. The hand fell away. "Go home, Miss Daniels," she said more gently. "Get help. I will do what I can for Emily, if there is anything to be done. But this is no place for you."

Her speech concluded, she went to the locked door and produced from her coat pocket a ring of keys which she began fitting into the lock, one after another. There were footsteps in the hall outside the kitchen. We both went perfectly still, but then they turned and retreated with a curse.

"Run," Miss Chase said over her shoulder. "It's only a matter of time before another one comes in."

I staggered to my feet and gave a last look at the door to the gardens, and safety. Back home, back to my father, back to everything small and familiar—and if something happened to Miss Chase, if I could have saved her or Emily or both and instead I ran away? To live with that, for all my days?

Oh, I would have made a poor pirate. I had known as much all my life. But perhaps, I could still be a brave woman.

I grabbed the poker from the floor, wincing at the glistening tip, and placed myself between Miss Chase and the hall door, listening intently for any approach. She looked at me, but continued trying keys.

"Are they all like him, then?" I nodded at the corpse.

"Not all," she muttered. "Some are common-or-garden cutthroats." She cursed under her breath. "How many bloody keys does he have?"

I said nothing, just focused on keeping my breath steady, on keeping a grip around the poker handle. Already, I saw it in my mind: if someone should come, I would swing as soon as the door opened, much as she had done. With luck, I would wind them before they knew I was there—

There was a sound of metal scraping and the lock dropped open with a clang.

Miss Chase eased the door open slightly, then, with a sigh, swung it wide. I took a breath before turning to look, but there was nothing: only a narrow spiral staircase going down into utter darkness, much like the one I had ascended upon my arrival. Indeed, I found myself glancing at the far wall to confirm that, yes, there was the door I had emerged from.

There was one difference: these stairs were marked by a brown smear that dappled each riser as far down as we could see.

"We need a lantern." Miss Chase looked around, then hurried to the hearth where one hung from a hook in the wall. She hunted around some more and produced a tinder-box.

From the hallway came distant footsteps drawing closer. They paused as someone shouted.

Swiftly, Miss Chase lit the lamp, then returned to me with a wary look at the hallway door. She kicked the lock into a corner, then handed me the lamp and pulled the pistol from my breeches, sliding it into her own.

"I am a competent shot," I said in a low voice.

"The last thing I need right now," she retorted, "is a country girl making free with my pistol." But her mouth was crooked up in the corner. "Last chance to run, Miss Daniels."

In response, I strode into the stairwell, descended a few steps, then held the lamp up while she drew the door to. And not a moment too soon; just as it shut completely, we heard the hall door open and heavy footsteps enter, followed by a low whistle. Miss Chase pulled the pistol free, waiting, her ear pressed to the door. After a moment, however, she grinned. She mimed stuffing her mouth full of food, then pointed the pistol at the stairs.

We began our descent.

CHAPTER XIV

Leviathan

*I*t seemed much farther going down than it had coming up. Around and around we went, following the small, shallow steps. The farther we went, the fainter the stain became, until at last it disappeared entirely, but the light picked up a scrap of linen clinging to a nail—a stained, stiff little thing, and somehow that was worse, much worse. I showed it to Miss Chase, who only nodded grimly.

We continued on.

The steps were dizzying, maddening. I tried to focus on maintaining my balance, readying myself for whatever might be waiting for us. For some time, there was only the sound of our shoes tapping against the stone and the regular sighs of our breathing—until, suddenly, came a roar of noise from above us. Miss Chase froze, looking up. "They found the body," she said. "Get to the bottom, quick."

I hurried then, moving down the slippery stairs as fast as I dared. The endless turning, turning. There were no more sounds from above—were they searching, were they arming themselves and readying to charge down upon us? Upon Miss Chase? For they had no way of knowing I was here. If I had run when I had the opportunity ... but my cowardly train of thought was interrupted as I suddenly came to a floor, stumbling from momentum. The lamp swung wildly in my hand as I righted myself and raised it high overhead.

We were in another cellar, similar to the one I had entered through, only this one was lined with racks and the racks were filled with assorted crates and small, squat barrels. Some were wrapped in oilskins, and plump sacks were piled atop the largest crates.

Before us, gaping and dripping, was the entrance to another tunnel, only this time it had clearly been created after the Hall was built. The stone was chiseled raggedly around its mouth, with rough beams reinforcing the opening. Cracks ran up through the mortar to the ceiling and beyond.

Right at its edge, where damp clods of earth spilled into the cellar, was a filthy wad of fabric. I picked it up and shook it out. A shawl, bloodied and mud-caked, its ends knotted tightly to make a kind of sling. The few delicate tassels remaining on its edges made my eyes well.

Emily.

"Do you think they took Emily down the tunnel?" I looked around. "Miss Chase?"

She was bent over one of the crates, feeling at the edges, then wiggled her fingers at me. "Let me see that poker."

It took but a moment for her to work the lid off and fling it aside, making a terrible clatter. Without a word, she began pawing through the wood shavings.

"Miss Chase?" I caught at her arm. "For God's sake, you'll bring them down upon us—" I broke off as she held a heavy sphere up to the lamplight, a long thick string dangling from it. "What is that?"

"Grenade." She frowned, poking one of the sacks with the poker. "Plus shot, and those barrels are gunpowder, I'm certain." She looked at me darkly. "We suspected Masterson and his brother were dealing in arms, the better to advance their cause. Or did he not regale you with his speech on how diplomacy is another word for cowardice?" When I only shook my head, she smiled bitterly. "It is not enough to simply protect England, it seems. He would have us conquer the world, no matter how many he must kill to make that happen."

"But why poor Emily, of all people?"

"I told you, Miss Daniels. He needs—"

Above us came the unmistakable sound of a door opening. "Chase?" The voice echoed down the staircase. "Is that you down there?"

"We must hide," I whispered urgently.

Miss Chase ran her fingers across the side of a crate, where LEVIATHAN was painted in grey paint. "If only there was something—paperwork, something that could serve as proof ..." she trailed off, then nodded at the tunnel. "Ladies first," she said more firmly.

Footsteps were descending, slowly, cautiously. Again, Sir Edward's voice came, closer this time. "It was neat work with Mister Kensington, Chase. I did not think you had it in you. It seems you have adapted to more than merely the dress of your chosen sex."

As I ducked into the tunnel Miss Chase caught my arm. She dipped the wick of the grenade into the lamp, then gave me a shove. "Run!" she whispered.

The voice, the first hints of light flickering on the stairwell, the burning wick—it all provoked me, and I ran. I ran faster than I knew I could, my legs unencumbered by skirts and my fears overcoming all propriety. Ahead of me, the tunnel was a few feet of lamp-lit earth leading into darkness. I could sense no fresh air ahead, no opening; still I ran blindly forward. It turned, it dipped, the walls shrank and opened up and shrank again. Behind me, I heard Miss Chase's panting breath, and far behind us both, the muffled sound of Sir Edward's voice barking orders.

The air seemed to fill with a sudden pressure. A moment later, a great booming noise echoed through the tunnel followed by a gust of hot, filthy air laced with debris. The force of the wind sent me to my knees and blew the lamp from my hand; Miss Chase fell atop me in turn. I was stung in a dozen places, I knew not by what or how. From behind us came screams, yells, and other, more terrible cries.

My breath would not come. The air tasted of smoke, smoke and a warmth that scalded my throat. Miss Chase groaned into my neck, and I carefully worked us both into a sitting position, gulping air and coughing. Her limbs were tangled awkwardly with mine and it took some doing to ease her upright. When I managed to trace my hands up to her face, I felt wetness.

"Keep moving," she rasped.

"We will," I said, surprised at the rough sound of my own voice. Before she could speak further, I wrapped her arm around my shoulders. My suspicions were borne out as her knees buckled, nearly sending us both to the ground again, but then she managed to steady herself, shaking her head over and over, her tousled hair brushing against my face. Slowly, carefully, we began an ungainly, hunched crabwalk along the tunnel, our heads lowered to avoid the worst of the smoke. In the darkness, the walls seemed to press in upon us, as we kept lurching against one or the other, and it was all I could to do keep from imagining that the very tunnel was collapsing upon us. I ignored the sounds behind me; surely, if we were so affected by the explosion, our pursuers would only be moreso. Besides, we had worries of our own. My eyes were watering from the smoke; if we didn't find air soon, we might suffocate.

The tunnel floor dipped beneath our feet. So focused was I on keeping Miss Chase steady, maintaining what little pace we had, and not envisioning ourselves entombed in dirt, that I did not notice the change at first. A sudden sharp decline, however, made us skid a few feet, and then I hesitated. Where was this leading to? What if we did, indeed, come to a dead end, or a collapsed section? There was not a soul who knew where we were, save those men who had followed us, and they would not care a whit about our fates.

"You should go ahead," Miss Chase muttered, as if she had been listening to my thoughts. "Get out, get help."

"Certainly not," I replied, though I heard the lack of conviction in my own voice.

"There is no point in both of us dying."

"There is no point in such talk." I began walking again. "We began this together, we shall finish it together."

She made a strange noise then. For a moment, I thought

she was having a seizure, and then I realized she was laughing, only the lack of air was making her gasp. "God save us from pretty country girls," she giggled.

I blushed, and for once I was thankful for the darkness.

"God save us from pretty, tack-sharp country girls," Miss Chase said again, still sniggering. "And their lovely smiles and their lovely curvy figures, and how they look at murdering bastards like they would eat them for dinner and take a stroll in the gardens after ..."

"Miss Chase!" I was blushing terribly now. I was also alarmed—was she hallucinating? "We must focus on our circumstances, not—not this."

"I am Joanna Chase and I am going to die in the arms of the prettiest woman I've seen in ages," she said, her voice wistful. "I am utterly focused on my circumstances."

"You're mad," I blurted out.

"And perverse, and unnatural, and I am blaming you for *everything*," she said. "Have you seen yourself in breeches?"

"Miss Chase, for God's sake—"

"Jo," she interrupted.

I swallowed. "Jo," I began, but then I could not think of what I meant to say. I was suddenly aware of every part of my body she pressed against, of the warmth of her breath on my neck. Indeed, I felt as if I could see her looking at me, though to look at her was to see only the black space we were in.

She stopped then, leaning heavily against me. "It's pointless," she mumbled.

"Oh." Still, I could not think. Her arms were around me. What was pointless?

"We have been walking too long; we should have come out somewhere by now. I am so, so sorry, Miss Daniels." Her voice was trembling; she sounded on the verge of tears. "I should never have brought you down here, I should have insisted you leave, I should have told you everything the moment we arrived—"

"Caroline," I interrupted.

"What?" She sniffled.

"If I am to call you Jo, you should call me Caroline." I touched her face gingerly. "You must have hurt yourself badly, you're saying the strangest things—"

Her lips pressed against mine. For a fumbling moment, my mouth was crushed by hers; but then instinct took over—oh! It was instinct and more, so much more. The feel of her, the taste of her. She tasted of a sweetness tinged with wine and salt, something that left me breathless and tingling, something that made me *want*, want beyond words. Her body pressed against mine and her hands tangled in my hair and every part of my body said *yes oh yes*.

We broke apart, gasping, and her hands fell away. "I'm sorry," she said breathlessly. "I, I just … Caroline?"

I licked my lips, tasting her still, trying to make my addled brain think, find words, do *something* …

"Caroline? Say something, please."

… when I realized I tasted not only Miss Chase—not only *Jo*—but salt. A faint breeze was running across my face, adding the slightest chill to my moistened lips.

"Jo," I whispered. "Jo, there's air."

I heard her lick something—a finger? After a moment,

she said wonderingly, "The sea?"

In response, I drew her arm around my shoulders once more. We moved with purpose now, pushing at the dirt that hemmed us in on all sides. With every step, the breeze felt a little stronger, the air a little cleaner. At one point, it gusted, and then we were hurrying as best we could, nearly falling over in our haste. A gleam of light showed us a curve, beyond it was light and flickering shadows and *life*.

We rounded the bend and halted abruptly, Jo making a little noise in her throat.

Before us was a circular opening showing the bay and an achingly blue sky, and between us and the water was part of a body, hanging upside down and swinging gently in the breeze. Hanging like meat. Naked like meat, bitten and gnawed like meat. There was what had clearly been a leg, and a hip, and a hint of a woman's sex—and then there was no more, save flesh so ragged, it dangled like the tassels on the shawl.

I turned away, breathing deeply, my head spinning. Emily. *Emily*.

"He usually throws the body into the sea," Jo said. "Why keep her here like this?"

"Because Emily was refused."

We both spun about, Jo drawing her pistol and aiming it at Sir Edward, who carefully stepped around the bend and directly in her line of fire. His bare, stubbled head was crusted with blood, his clothes sooty and ragged. A tear in his shirt revealed a mark on his chest, what looked very much like the odd-shaped sun branded on the crates. Behind him were two grubby men, one with a bloodstained face. More shadowy forms filled the tunnel behind them.

"It happens, on occasion," he said, his voice as smooth and as rhythmic as if we were back in our dining room. "Perhaps Emily lied about her parentage to me. Perhaps she was simply ignorant of her origins. But the offering was rejected." He smiled then. It was a cold smile. "Which means I'm in the hole one English female—but, thankfully, I always have at least one in reserve."

Instinctively I took a step backwards. Jo moved in front of me.

"You can shoot me, of course," he continued, spreading his hands. "But my lads will take care of you nonetheless—they'll have to, if they want my brother to pay up their wages. Nor will they be kind about it, for you destroyed their bonus back at the Hall."

"Then take me," Jo said. She pushed me back a little more, inching me closer to the edge of the tunnel mouth—and the rotting corpse dangling before it. "My blood is as good as hers, you told me that yourself."

"What are you doing?" I whispered. Now that we were close to the edge, I could see just how far we were from the water. Dark rocks jutted out below us. To fall would certainly spell our doom.

Rocks, the churning surf, and something else, something dark and vast and rippling …

"Why should I choose?" Sir Edward laughed, a loud, ringing guffaw that had a note of triumph. "It has already tasted Miss Daniels. The two of you will ensure England's supremacy at sea for months to come—and make our hold over our minister unbreakable." He angled his head, turning his dark gaze on me. "I am sorry it must end this way, Miss Daniels. You are a most charming woman. But everyone has to do their part for England."

Jo nudged me back again as she primed the pistol, aiming it unerringly at Sir Edward's head. "Jump," she whispered. Then, loudly, "You are absolutely correct, *sir*. We all must do our part."

"It is a poor day when the Crown sends a woman after the likes of me," he replied sadly, then snapped his head. "You know what to do."

His men pushed past him, eyeing the pistol warily. I took another step back, trying to think. The rocks were close to the cliff face—if we could somehow clear them—

Something moved, beneath the water. Wet black skin briefly broke the surface and disappeared.

The sight distracted me, and in that moment one of the men lunged for us. Jo fired and Sir Edward crumpled forward, tumbling against the second man, who fell against us all. I grabbed Jo and she grabbed Sir Edward and we all fell backwards.

Bright blue sky, limbs flailing. A fist struck me in the head. I twisted away and below us the waters parted and a great yellow eye appeared.

All, then, was black roiling reptile, twisting and writhing, and a hot gust of sour air that smelled like a thousand rotting fish. We struck not rock nor water but cold, leathery skin. My arms were locked around Jo's waist. She was kicking and flailing and I did not let go. I would die before I let go.

We skidded down the curve of what I knew to be a creature, more vast than anything I had ever seen, more vast than the Hall and its grounds, more vast than the sky above us. We skidded and fell into the churning icy bay, striking what felt like a serpent writhing. It slapped us away and we spun, choking and gagging, across the surface of the water and sank into white froth and waves that seemed to hit us from every direction. Jo was a dead weight in my arms. I kicked off my shoes and managed to push us both up, grabbing her chin to keep her head above water.

Bright blue sky and then a shadow fell over us. It reared up, water sheeting off its massive, glistening body as it spread several undulating limbs that blotted out the sun. It was serpent and squid and whale and ling and something else, something beyond imagining, and my mind jabbered *God God God.* From a tentacle, I saw a man dangling by one arm, shouting unintelligibly: Sir Edward. The limb rippled and sent his body sailing far out over the bay, and with a monumental effort the beast twisted and plunged after him. I glimpsed, at the center of its limbs, a vast, round mouth ringed with sharp teeth—

—oh it wasn't a sun at all, it had never been a sun—

—before the water rose in waves higher than the cliffs. Desperately, I pressed my mouth to Jo's and braced us both for the onslaught. Nothing, nothing, and then we were tumbling in the surf like so much flotsam, our clothes wrenching us about, our faces slapped apart. I gulped air and choked in panic, flailing and kicking, only to realize I was kicking against sand and rocks. Bracing my feet, I pushed us both above the water again, my arms digging into Jo's stomach; she coughed and vomited water, then began hacking violently.

We were nestled among the rocks at the far edge of the bay, right where the seawater funneled in. Spray after spray of crashing waves fell over us. I was trembling with cold and exhaustion; my body ached everywhere. The curving cliff face was now marred with a great divot, as if a cannonball had struck near the top. All that remained of the tunnel was a piece of wood jutting out at a sharp angle. Sir Edward, the men, Emily—all were gone. In the distance, I glimpsed a column of smoke rising into the sky. The Hall, I guessed.

In my arms, Jo shifted, then tried to get purchase on the slippery rocks. I helped her balance beside me. Her face was ashen, with blood running freely down the side of her face, and her whole body was shuddering with cold. Still, she smiled weakly when she looked at me.

"I stand corrected," she croaked. "There really is a bloody Leviathan."

CHAPTER XV

Confessions

There was no way to scale the cliff face from where we stood, nor had either of us the strength to try to fight the currents. Thus, it was some time before we were able to hail a fishing boat, which put out a dinghy as close to the rocks as it dared. We swam to that, slowly and laboriously, and it was with utter relief that we let the men pull us in. I did not bother to identify myself, and, indeed, if I looked anything like Jo, I was unrecognizable. Her hair was matted, her face coming up in bruises and crusted with blood, her bedraggled suit little more than a salt-encrusted ruin. Who would think to find Theophilus Daniels' daughter in such a state? Jo spoke for us both, saying we had gotten too close to the edge and the cliff had given way. That we were both women ensured we were treated with a wary suspicion; Jo's story, I knew, struck them as improbable, and they had probably seen the smoke from Harkworth Hall much as we had. We were consigned to the back of the boat with a cup of water apiece and a man watching over us. When they finally put in at the village, we were unceremoniously given the night to make ourselves scarce or they would inform the constabulary on us, and with that sending off, we limped from the village as quickly as we could, faint from hunger and reddened from the sun and brine.

As soon as we were a ways down the road, I tugged Jo into the thin stands of trees that ran alongside. She stumbled after me, sliding her hand into mine to steady herself, and though a small part of my mind warned against it, I could not but admit that it felt good.

"Isn't your house further on?" she asked.

"The Fitzroys are closest," I explained. "My father will be frantic. He'll have gone to Uncle Stuart straightaway to see if I was there."

She tugged me to a halt, leaning against a tree to catch her breath. "Caroline," she said, "I don't think we can trust them. Stuart Fitzroy has been dealing with Masterson for some time."

For a moment, I missed the import of her words, hearing only the *Caroline*. Then I realized what she was implying. "Uncle Stuart is no saint," I retorted, "and he has never seen a profit he wasn't inclined to take. But if you think he could somehow countenance all of, of that—monsters and, and *sacrifices*—" I took a breath. "He can be greedy, but he's not insane," I said more calmly.

"It was your Uncle Stuart," Jo replied in an equally calm voice, "who invited Masterson here and put you directly in his path."

Her words felt like a slap. I dropped her hand as if it were a live coal. "If he did, it was because he thought us a good match," I cried. "That is what fathers do here: they arrange matches for their daughters, good, respectable matches."

She gave me a look, but only stood up and began plodding forward again. I fell into step beside her, feeling completely overwrought. Could I say with absolute certainty that Uncle Stuart knew nothing? To have sway over a minister, the opportunities that would provide—could it turn even a man I thought of as family against all human decency?

How well did I know anyone?

"Caroline," Jo said.

Unwillingly I looked at her.

"Even if he had been what he claimed," she said. At my frown, she clarified, "Masterson, I mean. You would have been wasted on him, you know." She shook her head, smiling wryly. "Someone like you, sewing cushions and making tea? It would almost be as tragic as what happened to Emily."

I felt sick then, on top of everything else. I hadn't wanted to think of Emily. "I hardly think that is an appropriate comparison," I said.

"There are many ways to die," Jo said heavily. "Some die quickly and painfully; some take years, their life dribbling away ..." She took my hand and gave it a little squeeze. "Just—just promise me, if you do marry? Make sure it is someone who will let you be yourself. Someone who will let you *live*, as you deserve to live ..."

I meant to reply with something noncommittal, that would end the whole horrible conversation, but instead I blurted out, "I don't want to marry at all."

Jo looked at me, but said nothing.

"There is a—a book, in Uncle Stuart's library. A history of pirates." The words kept coming, why couldn't I stop them from coming? "There's a story in it, about two women, there was an etching of the one …" My face was burning, burning, as hot as if I was standing before an oven. "I wanted to *be* them. I wanted to be them so, so *badly*. I have never wanted to be a princess, or a wife. The very thought … I have met kind men, handsome men, and never once did I want so much as a kiss." My eyes were welling, but still the words would not stop. "I tell myself when the time comes I will find it pleasant, as all women do, or at worst it will just be another chore. I tell myself so many things … and I think only of the next day, the next chore, the next meal. But I don't want to marry, I don't want to at all."

I was weeping, I felt lightheaded, ill; yet the confession also felt good, as if some terrible, hidden wound was being drained at last. When Jo took my hand, I gripped it tightly, and she rubbed the back of my hand with her thumb.

"Was this Johnson's *History of the Pyrates?*" she asked.

I could not speak for weeping; I could only nod.

"I think we have a copy as well. I know I've seen it, I know exactly which etching you mean." Jo laughed. "Mary Read and Anne Bonny. There are worse guides for women."

I swallowed. "Diana thinks—"

"A pox on Diana Fitzroy," Jo burst out. She took a breath, then nudged me. "I would offer to marry you, you know, but I would probably get you hung." At my startled look, she smiled wryly. "I am an accomplice, after all, and it was made clear to me that if things went poorly, the Crown would use me as a scapegoat."

"After all this?" I cried, outraged. "They wouldn't dare!"

"His brother is still free," she said, "and we haven't a lick of evidence against him, save the word of two women." She nudged me again. "One of whom, it would be revealed, is the tribade daughter of a not-so-honorable London lawyer who was seen consorting with Thomas Masterson's libertine brother—and in breeches, Heaven preserve us. I'll be the face that launched a thousand broadsides."

Despite my swirling emotions, I couldn't help but smile. "Well, the rest could be forgiven, but the breeches—"

"I'm serious, Caroline." She stopped me completely, turning me until I faced her. "When all this comes to light, the news will be ugly and the gossip will be uglier. Whatever your plans for the future? There's no need for you to bring such ignominy down upon you and your father." She put an emphasis on *father*. "Once we get to the Fitzroys, show me to their door and then go home. I can keep your name out of it."

"I will decide my own fate, thank you very much," I retorted. I was suddenly, blindingly furious. I felt almost betrayed. "All my life," I burst out, "all my life people have decided for me. My father, my governess, the schools when they would no longer teach me, this age when it was decided I could not so much as cross a hillock alone, and now you …" I was weeping again. "Right now, I feel *alive*, truly alive, and you of all people would take that away from me?"

Jo hugged me. I started to beat at her but heard her hiss of pain and just gave myself over to sobbing instead. She said nothing; she simply held me, rubbing my back as I wept into her filthy coat. Only as my tears died away did I hear her soft voice hushing me. When at last I raised my face to hers, she was gazing at me, her expression unreadable. "You are certain?" she asked.

"Yes," I said.

And there was no further debate, then. Carefully, she slid her hand through the crook of my arm and we began walking once more. For a moment, there was nothing save ourselves, strolling through the sun-dappled woods like any two people out for a walk, the soft breeze easing our stinging faces and the air tinged with the perfume of the bluebells that cushioned our stockinged feet. Beyond the trees was the start of the meadows that ran to the bay, their green grasses tinged yellow in the afternoon sun, and in the far distance I could see the stone wall that marked the edge of the Fitzroys' land. The sight both gladdened and dismayed me. For the first time, it occurred to me just what a picture we made. All that I had confessed, that strange, wonderful kiss in the tunnel, it all seemed to be the acts of another Caroline, a more honest, daring version of myself. Now, with the prospect of the Fitzroys and my father before me, I felt that Caroline warring inside me with a smaller, more timid one who dreaded their censure.

But I had no time for such selfish worries. Jo's face was drawn, her pace had slowed, and I was struggling to support her with my own throbbing pains. The blow near her scalp had settled into an ugly, scabbed weal, and there was a strange whistling note in her breath. The field that lay between us and the wall, rather than drawing us closer to safety, seemed as immense as a desert to cross. Too, the wind increased as our path veered towards the coastline once more, sometimes leaving us breathless.

"Go ahead," Jo finally said, trying to prise her arm free of mine. "You'll make better time alone. You can send someone back for me."

"We are *not* separating," I replied. Grimly, I pulled her arm around my shoulders, ignoring my own body's aches.

"Caroline, be sensible."

"Now you want me to be sensible?" I found myself smiling despite everything. "There was no sense in my going to Harkworth Hall, there was no sense in your hiding me, and there was certainly no sense in going into the kitchen, much less the cellar, when we could simply have run away. I'm afraid, Miss Chase, that we are lost causes when it comes to sense."

She answered me with a soft laugh. "I knew you to be unusual from the moment I met you, Miss Daniels. Now I know you to be unusually foolish."

"That's the pot calling the kettle black," I replied, only to find myself giggling when she stuck her tongue out at me.

As we drew near the wall, we saw a figure appear before it, following its line. Halfway along the wall it stopped and lit a lamp, which it raised high in the air and swung back and forth, as if a beacon for us to follow. Confused, I shouldered Jo and kept moving—perhaps it was a servant? Perhaps they had put out a search party for me?

The lamp swung once more, then wobbled as the figure clearly leaned forward, peering at us. I waved and it cautiously waved back, then started walking towards us. As it drew close, I cried out in relief, "Uncle Stuart!"

For it was indeed Diana's father. He paused, clearly astonished at being hailed so. Never have I been so glad to see a person in my life. Here, at last, was aid and safety.

"Tell him nothing," Jo suddenly whispered.

"What?" I stared at her, astonished. "For God's sake, we must report what happened—"

"Tell him you were injured while walking, we brought you to the Hall, and we barely escaped the fire." She rattled off the story. "Just until a third party is present. *Please*," she added forcefully.

I could not debate the matter further, for we had reached Uncle Stuart. "Caroline!" he cried, raising the lantern to look at me. "And—Chase?" His tone changed to one of astonishment, and then, to my surprise, his expression became grim. "Well, this is a fine turn-up. Are you aware there has been a fire at the Hall and your good master might well be dead?" Without waiting for an answer, he turned back to me. "Your father has been mad with worry and here you are cavorting with this, this creature—how am I even to present you in such a state—"

"We were in that fire and we barely escaped with our lives," I interrupted coldly. All that had happened and he was upset about my appearance? "We need food, we need a surgeon, and we need to send for a constable."

Uncle Stuart gave me a long, considered look. "We certainly do," he said more calmly, then extended his arm towards the house. "Well. Let us get you both inside. I suspect this will be a most intriguing story."

Those last few yards to the Fitzroy home felt as long as all our walking beforehand. Jo was wheezing with pain now; I, in the meantime, was trying to give Uncle Stuart the half-truths she had asked of me. I had wanted to look for Emily, I explained, only I had tripped and fallen near the coast, where one of Sir Edward's men had spotted me. They brought me to the Hall, where Miss Chase kindly lent me a change of clothing. We had meant to send to my father this morning, but the fire had driven us out into the night. In the smoke and chaos, we had become lost, and only now returned.

Jo gave my shoulder a squeeze, but I could tell that Uncle Stuart didn't believe me. Still, he nodded and helped Jo over the threshold and into the quiet of the Fitzroy house. The familiar hallway with its candlelight, the smells of dinner cooking—it was impossible that he could be party to Sir Edward's madness, impossible that we could be anything but safe here.

"My servants are still out searching the countryside," he said, as he shut the doors behind us. "Your father is in the study. I'll have a word with the cook and then check the stables. If there's no lad to send for a surgeon, I will go myself."

I nodded and thanked him. Together, Jo and I worked the study door open and hobbled inside, and then my heart swelled. My father stood by the window, in a stance I knew too well: he was worrying terribly and trying to hide it. How many times had I seen him thus during my mother's confinement? When he turned at our entrance, the relief that overcame him was palpable, and I felt myself sagging in turn.

"Caroline!" he cried, rushing to us. "And Mister Chase! My God, what has happened? Are you hurt? My poor child!"

He made to embrace us but I laughingly pushed him back.

"We're both rather bruised, Father," I said. "Let's make, ah, *Mister* Chase comfortable first."

Together we helped Jo lie down on the chesterfield. She lay back with a sigh of relief that told me she was in far more pain than she had been letting on. If she had a hidden injury, one that was so long untreated … I looked at my father only to see him staring at me in astonishment and more than a hint of disapproval.

"Caroline," he began in a low voice, "you know I will support you whatever the circumstances, but we know nothing of this young man's family—"

"Father!" I felt my face burning. That Jo hid a smile only made it worse. "We have come from Harkworth Hall. We must send for the police and a surgeon at once."

"You were at the Hall? But there was a terrible fire, they thought everyone had been killed." He took an eager step forward. "What of Sir Edward? Did he too escape?"

His stricken tone made me wince. To him, Sir Edward was still a friend, yet to hear such concern after everything that had happened—

"We do not know what became of him," I snapped, and set myself to cushioning Jo's head with my coat, though she tried to wave me away.

My father, perhaps sensing something in my tone, quickly went to a side table and poured us each a glass of sherry. The liquid made me lightheaded, reminding me just how long it had been since either of us had eaten. "Have you had dinner yet?" I asked.

"No, I told Fitzroy I could not think of eating. I went to the Hall at first light when I saw the smoke. The place is a ruin, an absolute ruin. They had their hands full trying to search even the grounds." His face clouded over with pain and I laid a hand on his arm. "Where is Fitzroy? We need to send someone to the village and you must eat something, you look dreadfully pale."

"I think he was going to see to that, and then to the stables. He may have gone to the village for a constable."

"Oh, he won't find any there," my father said blithely. "They were all out at the Hall, and then I asked them to come here when they were done, in case you hadn't turned up yet."

Coming here! At once I was suffused with gratitude: for this parent of mine, for our escape from the Hall, for the knowledge that soon the whole terrible business would end. My eyes welled and I quickly turned away, lest I agitated my father further. "I will see if the cook can give us something," I managed to get out, and hurried from the room.

I was crossing the hallway when a soft voice called my name. I looked at the stairs to see Diana on the landing. Though I was relieved to see her, I realized that the sight of her no longer filled me with longing. What I felt was affection for an old friend, and nothing more—

I would offer to marry you, you know, but I would probably get you hung …

—but then I saw the pistol in Diana's hand.

"Diana?" My voice was a pathetic squeak. I took a step backwards, and another, as she descended the stairs. "Diana, what in God's name—?"

"Back in the study, Caroline." Her voice was shuddering, but the pistol was pointed unerringly at my chest. "I didn't want to have to do this," she added.

Slowly I backpedaled, my eyes never leaving her face. Behind me I heard my father and Jo conversing. They stopped abruptly when I entered. "Caroline," my father said gravely, "I think you need to sit down. Your, ah, *friend* has just made a most shocking confession … oh." I glanced over my shoulder to see him rise from the chesterfield, his face pale. "Diana," he said, but further speech seemed to fail him.

"Over there," Diana said, waving me towards the chesterfield. As soon as I was close enough, my father pushed me behind him.

"Diana," he began again. "Child. What is the matter? Surely, you're not afraid of us. Why, we're your oldest friends!"

Her eyes were glistening. "I am sorry, Uncle Theophilus," she said, her voice choked with emotion. "I am so very sorry."

"Sorry? You have nothing to be sorry for." My father gestured expansively. "Only tell us what is wrong. We'll do everything we can to help you."

I glanced helplessly at Jo only to find her looking at me through half-lidded eyes. The whole of her body spoke of feeling faint from pain, yet her lips moved silently.

Sword.

I followed her nod at my father's sword, hanging from his belt. I would have to reach around him, but Jo was close, if she could move quickly enough—

"You can start, my friend, by signing these."

We turned to see Uncle Stuart standing in the open garden doors. He, too, held a pistol loosely in one hand, and with the other he held out a sheath of papers. His own sword hung gleaming from his hip.

I glanced at Jo again, just catching her nod.

"What are those?" my father asked.

"Letters of transfer," Uncle Stuart replied. "They sign your estate over to me."

I gaped at him. My father flinched as if he had been bodily struck. "What? Fitzroy, what in God's name are you talking about?"

"I need your land, Daniels." He took a step into the room. "Things have gone too far, much too far, for us to turn back." His eyes flickered briefly to Diana's face. "You do not know what kind of men they are, Theophilus," he said in a low voice. "You do not want to know. Just sign these papers and I will let you and Caroline go free."

"And if we do not?" I asked.

"Then I will kill you all," he said heavily, "and blame it on Chase here, and those ruffians at the Hall. When they read your father's will, it will leave the land to his dear friend Stuart Fitzroy."

His words left me stricken. I turned to Diana, pleading. "Diana, you cannot countenance this!"

"Papa promised them," she said. A tear spilled over and wound its way down her powdered cheek. "He promised them the bay, Caroline. The money is already spent, we have no choice."

"For God's sake, Fitzroy," my father burst out. "You're a textile importer, not a murderer!"

"Not any more," Jo said.

We all looked at her; she had sat up and was glaring at Uncle Stuart. "We've seen it, Fitzroy. We've *seen* it. Do you honestly think you can wield that thing like a cannon, that you can use it for mere profit? How long before your daughter takes her turn, eh? Just a quick cut across the throat and into the sea. How much is her life really worth in this?"

"More than a scullery maid's," Diana retorted, while at the same time Uncle Stuart said, "I warned Masterson about you. The unnatural offspring of a pettifogger. He should have given you to the beast long ago."

He raised his pistol and I rushed between them. "Wait!" I cried. "We'll sign your papers. Won't we, Father?"

But when I turned to him, he was very pale; he seemed not to have heard me. "If I ever needed to sell," he said hoarsely to Uncle Stuart. "You've been telling me that for years now! If I ever needed to sell, and wouldn't it be better for Caroline to be in town. How long have you been planning this for?"

"Far longer than you can imagine," Jo said. Her arm was dangling over the side of the chesterfield—close to the hilt of my father's sword. But there were still the pistols and Uncle Stuart's sword to contend with, and my father to protect ...

"Father, please sit down," I said carefully. "Can he not sit, Uncle Stuart? Let me try and reason with him."

"No, no!" My poor father clutched at his head. "This makes no sense. How can this be happening? It makes no sense!"

There came a faint rumbling sound, as of a vehicle approaching. Uncle Stuart glanced over his shoulder, his expression uneasy.

"The constables!" My father's hands fell away and hope suffused his features. "Now we'll get to the bottom of this."

"You can dither all you like, Daniels," Uncle Stuart thundered. "Will you sign or not?" He jabbed the pistol at Jo. "Or should I begin with Chase here, to prove my intent?"

Diana suddenly pointed at the window, her face draining of color. "Papa!" she cried.

"Impossible," Uncle Stuart said, his gaze never leaving us. "We never sent for them."

"You did not, Fitzroy, but I did," my father declared proudly. "I spoke to them out at the Hall, before I came here. Now we'll find out what's really afoot." He held out his hand. "Give me those papers, Stuart. There will be no signing today."

I cannot say what exactly happened, then.

My father reached for the papers, as if to snatch them away from Uncle Stuart. At the same time, Jo seized my father's sword and Uncle Stuart took aim. She tackled him and a pistol fired. My father fell with a cry, but I was already running at Diana.

I threw myself against her and we tumbled to the ground. The pistol sailed from her grasp to shatter a windowpane as she struck me with a surprising amount of strength. The world went white and I rolled to my side. Her stricken face appeared before me as she slapped and punched me. Somewhere, a second pistol fired and plaster rained down on us. I seized one of Diana's arms and twisted it backwards, only to have her bring her other forearm down upon my throat, crushing the very air from me. Her face was contorted in a horrifying desperation. Everything began to swim—God I was *dying*—

And then Jo came up behind her and wrapped an arm around Diana's neck, dragging her off me. Diana kicked and tried to claw at Jo, and I wiggled backwards only to find the point of Uncle Stuart's sword at my throat. Jo screamed something—

And then constables rushed into the room, seizing us. The sword was taken from Uncle Stuart; my pale, shuddering father was borne away on a stretcher. Only later would I understand what one of the constables had said, shaking his head: that the second shot had been from Uncle Stuart's pistol. The shot which had so grievously wounded my father had been fired by Diana.

CHAPTER XVI

Changing Seasons

For several long nights, my father hovered between life and death. He had been shot in the hip, losing a quantity of blood and rending his leg all but useless. Far more debilitating was his subsequent fall, whereby he struck his head on the raised hearth of the fireplace. My world was reduced to his bedroom and the hallway outside, where I would listen to the surgeon's somber prognoses and Mr. Simmons' reports from the village. Of Jo, he could find no word. She had been spirited away by government agents, who had spoken darkly of outstanding warrants. Diana and her father had been similarly taken into custody and charged with several financial crimes as well as my father's assault. They were subsequently taken to London for trial, and apparently my statement was sufficient for the prosecution.

I could not think on how to press the matter further, and then I could not think at all, save to track each shallow breath from the shrouded bed, answer every minute pressure from the dear hand in mine. Mrs. Simmons, without prompting, set up a little cot in the room, and from time to time would stand over me while I obediently ate a few bites of food. I lost track of days, for the curtains were always drawn. I lost track of everything. Was it my father or my mother before me? Was I a grown woman, or a child once more? In my mind, the two scenes blurred until they were indistinguishable, forming one endless stretch of shadow and silence and, I, numb with grief.

Once, only once, I glimpsed from my father's window what appeared to be a suited figure standing in our gardens, gazing up at me. But by the time I reached the door, the phantasm was gone.

At last, my father's eyes opened. He seemed to know me, but when he tried to speak what came out was incoherent noise. I cried out for the surgeon and Mr. Simmons raced to fetch him. My father grew increasingly wild at his own tumbled reason, despite the efforts of Mrs. Simmons and I to comfort him. The surgeon arrived and gave him a sedative, then counseled me on a long and difficult recovery, in which my father might never regain his full faculties. I heard the surgeon's words; I answered them; I believed myself fully cognizant of their import. Only later that night, however, did I understand that my father's prognosis meant the end of that bolder, braver Caroline. There would be no more talk of marriage, but there would also be no further adventures, no more of that wild excitement, no more of that feeling of *alive* that I had experienced.

To ease my melancholy, I took to walking—just circling the house, in case I was needed, but each time walking farther, farther, five, ten, twenty circuits at a time, clockwise and counterclockwise. Building my endurance, or so I told myself, though I had nothing in the future to endure. It was with a bittersweet pang that I saw, one late summer morning, a lapwing careen overhead, and heard its peculiar cry. Each day after there were more birds, and more, until the air was as full of song as it had always been. It seemed an end to something, a diminished return to the life I had known.

I thought all this and I kept walking, step after step, circuit after circuit.

Thus, summer passed into autumn. My father's recovery was as slow and difficult as the surgeon predicted, with long stretches of anguish and frustration punctuated by tiny achievements: the hard first syllable of *Caroline*, the steady movement of spoon to lip. I tried to take as much joy as I could from these milestones, yet my heart sank every time I looked out the window and saw the falling leaves that blew across our grounds.

Without the pressing fear of my father's illness, the brief events of the summer began to haunt my sleep. Again and again I felt that strange, wonderful kiss in the darkness, the slide of Jo's thumb across my hand and what I knew now to be the sweet sensation of being *understood*, in some deeply important way. Again and again I saw the monster rising over us, and Sir Edward's body so dwarfed by those vast limbs, his jittering body becoming the remains of Emily, which became Diana's twisting blows as she tried to kill me … too, with hindsight, I began to wonder at aspects I had ignored in the peril of the moment. What of Thomas, the brother? How did he figure in Sir Edward's schemes? How many more were involved in the cult of the so-called Leviathan? What reasoned explanation could account for the creature's existence, and what reaction did a woman's blood and body provoke that Sir

Edward had found so desirable?

Sometimes I found myself gazing at where the water lay, just past the trees ringing our house, and wondered where the beast had gone. To the coast of Europe, to lay waste on command? Or had it retreated to some deep, dark recess in the cold seas? There was no one I could speak to about it, save for Jo.

In a renewed effort to reach her, I sent Mr. Simmons to the post office to review their directories and he returned with an address for Chase, Atkinson, and Wood, Attorneys. Using that address, I wrote to Mrs. Matthew Chase, asking if Joanna was safe and well. When at last Simmons handed me the envelope with its unfamiliar handwriting, my heart leapt, but to read the letter felt as if I were losing yet another beloved figure in my life.

Miss Daniels,

With regards to your letter inquiring after Joanna Chase, I must ask that you never invoke her name again. I have no such child.

Mrs. Matthew Chase

It was done, then. Whatever hope I had of somehow ascertaining Jo's fate, or even seeing her again, was gone. And even if I had contacted her, what would have been the point? To invite her to stay with me and help nurse my father? It was no life for a creature such as her; I knew this in my heart.

When the carriage arrived that afternoon, I was feeling

particularly resigned. At first, I ignored the knocking, until I remembered that Mrs. Simmons had gone after her husband as he had forgotten the shopping list. With a quick glance at my sleeping father, I hurried down the stairs, not even thinking about my dishevelment. The surgeon was used to seeing me in such disarray—

Only to stop, bewildered, at the sight of the plainly dressed, fidgeting woman on my doorstep, my mind unable to comprehend the shy, hopeful expression that met mine.

"Am I that wretched in skirts?" Jo asked.

In response, I threw my arms around her neck and burst into tears. She hugged me back tightly, nearly pulling me off my feet. "Caroline," she breathed into my hair.

"You're all right." I was crying so hard I could barely form the words. All that I had refused to consider during these long weeks, it all came pouring out. "I thought you were dead, I thought you had been shipped to a colony, I thought—"

She hushed me. "I'm so sorry," she said, her voice as choked as mine. "They wanted to wait until the trial was over before letting me contact you—"

"I even wrote to your mother!" I burst out.

At that she laughed, drawing back and wiping at both our faces. "And received a most unhelpful reply, I'm sure."

I couldn't speak, I couldn't let go of her. I couldn't stop looking at her.

"I thought the dress might prove easier for your father," she said, glancing down at herself. "Though I'm afraid to ask how he fares? They said he was recovering, but I didn't dare hope …"

I was smiling through my tears and yet my heart sank at

her words. Never had I felt so many emotions at once, and unable to name a one. "He can speak if he is careful, and the surgeon thinks he might walk a little with practice. I—" I broke off, bowing my head. "Perhaps you should not have come," I mumbled.

"What do you mean?" She ducked down, trying to catch my gaze. "Caroline. If you do not want—I mean, I hadn't planned that we … that you and I …"

"I cannot leave him," I said. My throat was closing painfully. "I cannot leave him, Jo. Not anymore."

"Ah." The sound came out almost guttural. For a moment, she was silent. I dared not look at her. At least I knew she was all right. At least I knew, now.

"Is this Miss Daniels, then?"

I jerked up to see a man standing by the plain black carriage. I had not realized she had a companion. He was small and slight, dark-skinned, with eyes made unreadable by spectacles and his tricorn pulled low. His suit was as luxurious as any I had ever seen, and his walking stick was topped with what looked like gold.

"If you could give us a moment," Jo said over her shoulder.

"I do need to get back—"

"A moment," she interrupted, her voice cold.

With a shrug he turned and strolled a little ways down the drive where he stopped once more, tapping one gloved finger against the shiny gold.

"You are being sent away," I whispered.

"Quite the contrary." She took my hand in hers, holding it as if it were something fragile. "I do not want to say too much.

I want you to hear him without prejudice." She squeezed my hand as I started to speak; I realized with a start that she was trembling. "The choice is yours, Caroline Daniels. It is entirely yours. Just know that, no matter what? I would—I would like to stay nearby, if I could. I would like to know you better, I would like—but I've said too much," she finished in a rush. "You must decide."

I felt utterly bewildered. "You would stay? Even with ..." Suddenly I heard in my mind the rest of her words. "Wait, what do you mean, decide? Decide what?"

But she only squeezed my hand again, then gestured to the man. "He needs to return to London tonight, thus he would speak with you now," she said more formally. "Know, too, that you do not have to decide anything today. You do not have to do anything save what you think best for *you*."

She released my hand and started to step back, but I caught at her arm. "Promise me," I said. "Promise me you'll stay right here."

At my words her whole face lit up. She smiled warmly at me. "I promise."

I knew then I was to move, to turn and speak to this stranger, yet I could not stop looking at her. She met my gaze unflinchingly, but I could feel her trembling beneath my hand, and it seemed that somehow we said much to each other, though neither of us uttered a word aloud.

"Bloody hell, Caroline," she finally whispered.

I burst into giggles, a nervous relief washing over me. Jo started snickering in turn. "We really must do something about your swearing," I said.

At that her smile became something else, something far more sly, and I felt an answering tremor deep in my belly. "You are more than welcome to try, Miss Daniels," she purred.

"Miss Chase?" The man's voice brought us up short. We both turned to see him holding up a large watch, his foot tapping.

Jo laughed again and angled her head. "Go on, then. Before he becomes properly cross."

"Should I fetch a pistol?" I inquired.

She gave him a considering look. "I *think* you should be safe," she said. "But do feel free to slap him if he offends."

At her encouraging smile, I turned at last to this strange visitor. As I crossed the drive I noticed how utterly blue the sky was, crossed by a hawk lazily surveying the grasses. The last week had been nothing but cold rain. It seemed somehow important that the day was so perfectly glorious.

As I drew close, I glanced up at the windows, and for a moment I thought my father was gazing down upon me; but it was just a shadow crossing the glass.

Upon inspection, the strange man was older, closer to my father in age than myself, but with a lithe bearing and bottomless eyes that seemed to look right through me. He made no motion to remove his hat, and instead of kissing my hand, he gave it a hearty shake.

"Miss Daniels," he said warmly. "I am delighted to meet you at last. Perhaps we can walk a ways together? I have a proposal for you."

With a last look at Jo, I slipped my hand through his crooked arm and we began strolling across the field, dried leaves crackling under our feet. "You have the advantage of me," I said, "for while you know my name, I do not know yours, nor anything about you."

"My last name is Smith," the man replied. "You can call me that. I have no title as such. I report only to His Majesty, and only on very select subjects."

"Such as Sir Edward Masterson?"

"Indeed." He tapped his cane rhythmically on the soft grass as we walked, an odd, muffled staccato to our measured steps. "Though, please do not call him 'Sir.' The man was never honored for anything in his life. You did us a service this summer, both in witnessing the creature and in discovering at least one of his intimate circle, Mister Fitzroy." He shook his head. "Ancient beasts in our waters, young women being treated like slop, fanatics exercising their perversities to the fullest … we live in strange times, Miss Daniels, with dark currents that press against us unceasingly."

"But surely there is no more cause for concern," I said. "Sir—Mister Masterson is dead, his stockpile of munitions is destroyed, and the beast has vanished."

"We have thought Edward Masterson dead before," Mr. Smith said. "I will not trust in such a pronouncement until I have seen proof." He gestured with his cane, as if sketching the outline of a corpse. "Meanwhile we still have the brother to contend with. Thomas Masterson recently moved his trading company farther down the coast—perhaps to put distance between himself and events at the Hall. He owns ships, deals with other nations, has amassed his fortune and influence with unusual rapidity … and recently, he lost a ship in a well-trafficked portion of the North Sea, an area that should have been easily navigable."

"He lost the entire ship?"

"With a full cargo, possibly including slaves. All hands were lost." He stopped, looking at me with a somber expression. "Considering what you and Jo witnessed, I am wondering if the younger Masterson is perhaps feeding the creature in a more brutish manner. He has used his brother's tactics as well—he, too, seems to provoke all manner of young women to simply vanish." His tone was bitter. "There are a great number of people still suffering at their hands, Miss Daniels. I want to end this."

I was shivering, though the sun was unusually warm. "Mister Masterson said the beast protected England, and he had a minister at his command," I said. "Perhaps you are looking in the wrong place, if you wish to end this?"

"Would that it were so simple." He gently tugged on my arm and we began walking again. "I am assembling a case against the Mastersons' minister friend. But I dare not make any official inquiries into Thomas Masterson before I make my move, and in the meantime, how many more will be lost to this scheme?"

"You want Jo to stop him," I said in a small voice.

"I want Miss Chase to find proof of *any* crime, even fraud, even that he's boarded up a bloody window," Mr. Smith said forcefully. "Anything that can get him in irons and put a stop to his activity. We have one small blessing in this: she has not yet met the younger Masterson. With a new name and her understanding of at least part of their scheme, she will be uniquely positioned for this task—and once he's out of the way, I can end this cult for good and hunt that beast to the bottom of the sea if necessary." He took a breath. "But, of course, all of this depends on you."

I looked at him, startled. "I don't understand."

"Miss Chase has made you part of her contract, Miss Daniels." He tucked his cane under his arm and pulled a folded paper from inside his coat. "That is, she has made you and your father part of her contract. She wants to bring you both with her to the town where Thomas Masterson has relocated. Your story will be that you are a married couple in genteel poverty, struggling to care for your ailing father. The local populace will be more likely to confide in you, and she will be better able to convince Masterson of her desperation." He smiled at me. "Love and poverty, Miss Daniels. The ingredients of many a man's downfall."

I took the paper from him and held it up to the sunlight. That copperplate hand. I had trouble reading the words, so blurred did my vision become.

she has an intuition which I lack, and matches me for courage save when she surpasses it. I think she would not only be an asset to this inquiry, she may well be that which tips it in our favor

I swallowed back my tears. My hand was trembling. I felt something small and warm and glowing burst forth, a kind of happiness I had never felt before.

"You would, of course, pretend to be married," Mr. Smith said. "It would mean cohabitating as such. Indeed, she has even stipulated that your joint surname must be Read, though

I have no idea why. If these terms pose any obstacle …"

Mary Read. "No," I said, biting my lip at the tremor in my voice. "No obstacle."

He looked at me, then took a step closer, so close his hat blotted out the sunlight. "I want to be absolutely clear, Miss Daniels. My only interest is in the service you can do me, and by extension, His Majesty," he said in a low voice. "However, if I can use you in a way that makes you happy? So much the better."

I stopped then, for I could not see the path before us. Mr. Smith pressed a handkerchief into my hand and I dabbed my eyes. I took my time and he waited patiently, as if he understood that I was trying to reason through all he had proposed.

Finally, I said, in a calmer voice, "My father is not well."

"Indeed." He laid both hands atop his cane, leaning forward.

"If I am caring for him, how can I—"

"Make no mistake, I want no more Harkworth Halls, Miss Daniels. It took a great deal on my part to smooth that mess over, and there are still a few drunks in your village muttering about things they saw. We were lucky not to have a public panic on our hands." His expression was grim. "I want something to arrest Thomas Masterson on and *nothing* more. Your job will be to make Miss Chase plausible. Her job will be to find proof of something criminal and leave at once. Is that clear?"

"Quite," I replied, matching his firm tone. "I would want my own salary, of course."

He blinked at me from behind the spectacles, but said nothing.

"And I would want access to a physician as well as a surgeon at all times. This journey is to benefit my father's health, not injure him further."

Again he blinked.

"And," I continued, warming to my newfound role, "I will reserve the right to end our activities at any time. If I believe the danger is too great to myself, my father, *or* Jo, I will return us *all* here at once, whether or not you have your information, and we will suffer absolutely no repercussions from you or any other agency. Is that clear?"

He blinked once more, then sighed heavily. "Quite," he snapped, crooking his elbow at me. "Shall we?"

But I held up my finger. "I have one further request."

"Is it a request or a demand?" His voice was nearly a growl.

"Let us say a pertinent request?" I was smiling now. "I was a liability at Harkworth Hall. I do not wish to be so again. I want someone to teach me how to fight. How to throw a punch, handle a knife, and improve my aim. I need to know these things."

"Your job," Mr. Smith began, bristling, "is to simply *look* the part—"

"And I pray to God I will never need these skills," I interrupted smoothly. "But needs must where the devil drives."

He glared at me a moment longer, then jabbed his elbow at me. I took it with a benign smile. Indeed, the world seemed an even warmer, brighter place than before. The sky seemed to have deepened its hue, the sun dazzling, the bare trees seemingly upraised in celebration, every blade of withering grass as beautifully colored as if painted by a master.

I was alive.

"As to the latter," Mr. Smith said after a moment. "Miss Chase is well-versed in your requirements. She can easily undertake your tutelage."

We were rounding the corner of the house. I smiled almost helplessly at the sight of Jo pacing on the front step, wrenching irritably at her skirts. "Mister Smith," I said warmly, "I must insist that it be anyone *but* Jo. What kind of marriage would we have, if we began with fisticuffs and knife fights?"

He laughed then, a deep, booming laugh that seemed at odds with his small stature. "A most unusual one, but I would wager better than many."

I gave him a sideways look, but he merely stopped and held out a hand. "I will send a contract in a few days along with your instructions," he said. "I would say it has been a pleasure, but I think you got the better end of this bargain."

We shook hands and without further ado, he turned on his heel and climbed into the carriage, slapping its roof even before he had shut the door. I turned to see Jo lurching down from the porch, her expression one of hope and anxiety. Before I knew what I was doing, I was running towards her, running with full heart and lungs and the whole of my body alight, as I had not done since I was a little girl.

Miss Chase and Miss Daniels return in

Leviathan

ACKNOWLEDGEMENTS

Some believe writing is a solitary activity, but they are utterly, utterly wrong. This book would not have been possible without the help of many. Laurel Amberdine, Sian Jones, and Rhonda Parrish gave me thoughtful, and at times painfully honest, feedback. Kat Howard patiently and repeatedly nudged me back on course as my first draft tripled in size and complexity. Anna Genoese gave me a thorough review and some last-minute suggestions, and Charlotte Ashley gently relieved me of as many grammatical crutches as I could bear to part with. The cover and interior are the work of Najla and Nada Qamber respectively, and I will say it again for the seats in the back: *mea culpa,* Najla, you were absolutely right.

I am fortunate to have a supportive and caring family who have cheered me on throughout my writing efforts, and a spouse and two cats who endured many late dinners with a minimum of dark looks and impatient pacing. Never underestimate hungry loved ones as a motivation for finishing your day's work.

ABOUT THE AUTHOR

L.S. Johnson was born in New York and now lives in Northern California, where she feeds her cats by writing book indexes. Her stories have appeared in such venues as *Strange Horizons, Interzone, Long Hidden: Speculative Fiction from the Margins of History*, and *Year's Best Weird Fiction*, and she has been nominated for a Pushcart Prize and longlisted for the Tiptree Award. Her first collection, *Vacui Magia: Stories*, won the 2nd Annual North Street Book Prize. To learn about new stories, upcoming appearances, or to be on the list for advance review copies, sign up for her newsletter at www.traversingz.com.